CREED

Book One

Kathleen Kelly
USA Today Bestselling Author

Creed
Royal Bastards MC Jacksonville, FL - Book One

Kathleen Kelly
USA Today Bestselling Author

ISBN: 978-1922883025

Editing by Beyond DEF Publishing Services
Proofreading by Beyond DEF Publishing Services
Book design by Swish Design & Editing
Cover design by Lucian Bane
Cover Image Copyright 2022
First Edition 2022
Copyright © 2022 Kathleen Kelly
All Rights Reserved

DEDICATION

To the readers who love MC, this is for you.
I hope you like it.

Below is a list of the other club chapters listed in this book and their authors.

In order of appearance:

Miami, FL – **Addison Jane**
Tampa, FL – **KE Osborn**

FOURTH RUN

B.B. Blaque: Royally Malevolent
Morgan Jane Mitchell: Royal Road
Crimson Syn: Wrecked from Malice
Glenna Maynard: Claiming the Biker
Liberty Parker: Property of Wrecker
Amy Davies: Fighting for Una
Addison Jane: His Rival
Erin Trejo: Trek
Misty Walker: Petra's Biker
Chelle C. Craze & Eli Abbott: Wiley AF
KL Ramsey: Dizzy's Desire
Nikki Landis: Twisted Devil
M. Merin: Wolfman
Kristine Allen: Sabre
J. Lynn Lombard: Derange's Destruction
Deja Voss: Forbidden Bruises

Darlene Tallman: Brick's House
Nicole James: Keeping the Throne
Shannon Youngblood: Kingdom and Kourt
India R. Adams: Praying for Thunder
Jessica Ames: Into the Dark
J.L. Leslie: Worth the Pain
Nicole James: Climbing the Ranks
Elle Boon: Royally Judged
J.L. Leslie: Worth the Trouble
Kristine Dugger: Familiar Taste of Poison
Kathleen Kelly: Creed
K.E. Osborn: Alluring Abyss
Murphy Wallace: Injustice and Absolution
Ker Dukey: Havoc
Dani Rene: A Beautiful Monster

Royal Bastards MC Facebook Group -
https://www.facebook.com/groups/royalbastardsmc/
Website- https://www.royalbastardsmc.com/

Royal BASTARDS CODE

PROTECT: The club and your brothers come
before anything else and must be protected
at all costs.
CLUB is **FAMILY**.

RESPECT: Earn it and give it. Respect club law.
Respect the patch. Respect your brothers.
Disrespect a member and there will be hell to pay.

HONOR: Being patched in is an honor, not a right.
Your colors are sacred, not to be left alone, and
NEVER let them touch the ground.

OL' LADIES: Never disrespect a member's or
brother's Ol' Lady. **PERIOD.**

CHURCH is **MANDATORY.**

LOYALTY: Takes precedence over all, including well-being.

HONESTY: Never **LIE, CHEAT,** or **STEAL** from another member or the club.

TERRITORY: You are to respect your brothers' property and follow their Chapter's club rules.

TRUST: Years to earn it... seconds to lose it.

NEVER RIDE OFF: Brothers do not abandon their family.

CREED

Chapter

CREED

Sitting opposite the head of the Diablo Cartel, I can see why they appointed a woman. People think she's weak, but Camilla Sanchez is as cold and ruthless as they come. She looks like a goddess, but when she smiles, she looks like an alligator contemplating its next meal. Giving Camilla his best smile and openly ogling her body, Scout looks at her as if she's his next conquest. Occasionally, Camila glances at him, distaste plastered across her beautiful features.

"I hate to repeat myself," she throws her silky black hair over her shoulder, "but you were short on the last shipment. Again."

We're in her office inside an old warehouse on the outskirts of town. It's one of those places near the glades where men in boats can easily take bodies out and feed them to the gators. Camilla often meets us in town, but today she's making a point.

Leaning forward, I tap my finger on the rough, wooden surface of the table, scarred with deep gashes, I assume were created by an axe or a machete. Probably both.

"Then it was short when we got it."

Camilla draws in a deep breath and shakes her head, her ruby-red top lip curled in a snarl. "It wasn't."

Smiling, I tap my finger again. "I'm not doing this fucking dance with you, Camilla. The fucking shipment was short. We don't skim. I'm not a fucking idiot."

Her eyes travel to Scout. "No, *you're* not."

Scout's eyes bulge and he shakes his head. "I wasn't even on the run."

Camilla sighs loudly and folds her arms across her chest. "I'm not paying you the full amount. The shipment was short. It's coming out of your end."

"Like fuck it is." I slam my fist on the table, toppling her glass of water.

Camilla's eyes blaze, and she stands, brushing the water off her tight-fitting black skirt. "Fuck!" She glances over my shoulder at one of her men.

I roll my eyes. "I can cross this table and bury my knife in your chest before the fucker reaches me."

Camilla freezes, her gaze settling on me.

"It wasn't us." I shrug dismissively. "We've been in business a long time. I give you my word, on my club, we aren't stealing from you."

It's not a promise I make lightly. Camilla knows if I'm willing to swear on the club, I'm not trying to swindle her. Nevertheless, her heroin has been short twice. The only men I put on the run are clean—no drug users. It reduces the risk they'd be tempted to dip into the stash, but it doesn't mean one might have decided to make some money on the side. Unlikely, but you never really know someone, do you?

Camilla looks at her man behind me and flicks a hand, signaling him to stand down. She turns, places her hands on her voluptuous hips, and stares out over the glades. Her shoulders rise and fall as she takes a deep breath, clearly trying to decide her best course of action. Camilla is in charge of the Florida arm, but she answers to her father, Mateo, and he will *not* be pleased with her.

"You've been in talks with the Khans. Prove your loyalty to us, we don't want you running their crystal meth. Agree to this and we'll overlook the infraction ... *this* time."

I stand and bark out a laugh. "The Khans have approached us. We're having a conversation, but our deal with you has nothing to do with them."

Slowly, Camilla turns around, her head slightly tilted. Her eyes meet mine as she lifts her chin. The next thing I know, a gun is shoved into my ribs and a hand lands on my shoulder.

Camilla smiles. "Agree to my terms."

Scout moves to stand, but one of her men slams his head to the table's surface and holds a knife to the back of his head.

"You kill me or him and you'll start a war. Mateo and your brother, Gabriel, won't be pleased. My men will fuck up your trade routes. You don't want to do this over two shipments being short, Camilla," I growl through gritted teeth.

"You've got some balls on you, Creed." Camilla leans forward, putting both hands on the table. Her breasts strain against the fabric of her jacket, and I know she's doing it on purpose. I'm probably one of the few men who have turned her down, but I like my women to have a bit of warmth about them, so I don't have to worry they're going to kill me in my sleep. "Agree to my terms and we all walk away happy."

Dropping my head to my chest, I relax my body. My eyes lock with Scout as he struggles against his attacker. I shake my head, and he stops moving.

"Well?" Camilla's voice is sweet as sugar.

My top lip curls, and I twist my body to the side. The gun fires, but it's facing toward Camilla. She flinches but doesn't move as it sails past her and shatters the window behind her. The woman has bigger balls then some men I know. I shove the gun farther away from myself and headbutt the ape behind me. He cries out in pain, then I raise my ring-clad fist and smash it into his already bleeding nose. The gun clatters to the floor.

We only have a few moments before more of Camilla's men come running through the door, but I have to free Scout. When I'm sure the man who had me pinned is down, I turn to look at Scout. He's bleeding from his neck, but his captor is down, his dead eyes staring at the ceiling as blood oozes from the knife embedded in his chest. Bending, I pick up the gun and toss it to Scout.

"Door!" I say thunderously as I draw my hunting knife from my belt and stalk around the table toward Camilla.

She backs away from me, but Camilla doesn't scare easily. Even as I close the distance between us, her eyes flit back and forth as she calculates her next move. We both know if I kill her, I'm as good as dead.

Raising my knife, I bury it in the wall beside her head. "Call off your men."

"Fuck you," she hisses.

"Camilla, we aren't fucking skimming, and the deal with the Khans isn't done. They won't be infringing on your territory. We made sure of that. They're only passing through, their meth is headed for Michigan. We'd never shit where we eat. It's another stream of income for us. The Khans agreed to keep it out of Florida."

"But it's *in* Florida!" Camilla screeches, her beautiful features twisted into a mask of contempt.

"Yes, but it's not the Khans who are running it, and you know it. Besides, Florida isn't your biggest money maker. Hell, it's not even your second biggest. Nebraska and Indiana win those spots, so what's this really about?"

Her eyes widen.

There's a reason I'm President of my chapter. I pay attention to everything, and something isn't right. We run drugs for the Diablos, and I make it my business to know the ins and outs of it all. We also run guns and whores and anything fucking else that will make money for my club.

With defiance in her eyes, Camilla says, "Your last two shipments *were short*."

With my fist still wrapped around the handle of my knife, I raise my other hand, place it on her throat, and begin to trace circles with my thumb at the base.

"How can I fix this, Camilla?"

Her tongue darts out, wetting her lips, and her eyes drop to my mouth. "You can't. You've killed two of my men."

Staring at her lips, I say, "No, only one, and he sliced up Scout pretty good. I think we're even."

Camilla's breath hitches as I release the knife and cup her breast. "Stop."

Smirking, I roughly massage her bosom and push myself against her. "I don't think so." Her eyes widen, but her body betrays her as she arches against me. "Hold the door, Scout!"

Leaving the knife in the wall, I grab Camilla by the shoulders and move her toward the table, bending her over it. Forcibly, I spread her legs with my knee and lift her skirt over her ample ass. Once I have her in position, I unhook my belt, release the button and zipper on my jeans, and lower myself over her, my cock between her ass cheeks.

"Tell your men to stand down."

"No."

Sliding my hand across her ass and between her legs, I'm surprised to find her dripping wet. Camilla's arousal coats my fingers. "If you tell your men to stand down, I'll fuck you hard."

Camilla pushes backward, trying to impale herself on my cock. Looking at Scout, I chuckle. He's always wanted to fuck her, and I've never been interested. Scout shakes his head as he struggles to keep the door closed. His blood coats the side of his neck and drips down onto the floorboards.

"Do you really want your men to burst in here while I'm fucking you? You'll look weak. Get them out of here."

"I'm fine! It was a misunderstanding! Leave us!" yells Camilla.

The pounding on the door stops, and Scout slides

to the floor holding his hand to his neck. He shakes his head in disbelief as I fill her with my cock.

She moans as I move in and out of her. I'm eager to get this over with. Fucking Camilla is the last thing I want to do. I don't like to mix business with pleasure, and I've been warned she's a jealous bitch. I belong to no one. I fuck who I want, when I want. This doesn't mean I'm hers, and I need Camilla to understand this.

Wrapping her long hair around my fist, I pull her up as I pound into her. Camilla's neck is bent back at what I'm sure is an uncomfortable angle.

"You mean nothing to me. This is fucking, that's all. You're an itch I needed to scratch and when it's done, we'll go back to the way we were."

Her pussy contracts as she grunts in satisfaction. "Y-yes," Camilla whimpers. "Ahh, yes." Her body shivers as her orgasm washes through her.

When I'm sure she's finished, I pull out and release her. Camilla sighs, clearly enjoying rough play, not that I'm surprised. My cock is hard, and I haven't blown my load, but the thought of continuing makes me want to vomit. Turning away, I tuck myself back into my jeans and refasten them.

This isn't how I saw things going today. I knew Camilla would want compensation for the missing bricks, and I'm sure the problem is on her end, not ours. Her brother is jealous she's in charge here in Florida, so my money is on him.

Sucking in a breath, I turn around to face her. She's sitting on the table, legs crossed, with a cigarette in her perfectly manicured hand. Her red nails match her lips, reminding me of blood and death.

"I'm deducting 2k from your payment."

Scowling, I point at her. "No, you're fuck–"

"Stop. I'm deducting 2k from your payment, but I'll make it up to you with the next shipment. I need to keep my father happy. If he's happy, I'm happy. If I'm kept happy," she smiles, sucks on her cigarette, and flicks ash to the floor, "this arrangement will continue. After today, I see a long, long partnership. Don't you?"

"This," I gesture from my cock to her body, "isn't going to happen again. Take your 2k, but it wasn't us. I'll prove it. Count the bricks, do it twice. When it gets to us, we'll do a count too. We'll do it the whole way, from person to person. Whoever is skimming will get caught. I'll put a bullet in them myself."

"No, if it's not you or your men, my father will want to make a show of them." Camilla smiles and takes another drag of her cigarette.

My stomach turns over. Mateo is famous for filling a tire with gas and putting it around whoever has betrayed him before lighting it. The person runs around screaming, the stench of scorched flesh and burning rubber filling the air as they die painfully.

When we went into business with Mateo, he invited me to his compound in Mexico and showed me what he does to those who disappoint him. It's the sickest, scariest shit I've ever seen. The woman was his lover, and she'd been caught with one of his bodyguards. They'd castrated the bodyguard before doing the same to him.

I'm not that man. I'm not that stupid.

My cock goes limp, and I nod. "Fine."

Camilla hops off the table, straightens her skirt, and places a hand on my chest. "Yes, you are."

Stepping away from her touch, I pull my knife from the wall and return it to its sheath as I stalk toward Scout. Holding out a hand to him, I help him to his feet. He grimaces as he stands. His hand is coated in blood as he holds it to his neck.

"See you in a month," Camilla calls out.

Opening the door, I see a wall of men with their guns out. "See you in a month," I reply loudly.

They drift out of the way as Scout and I move out of the warehouse and head to our bikes. I toss Scout an old t-shirt from one of my saddlebags.

"Here, put some pressure on your neck."

"I'm worried I'm going to bleed out."

Laughing, I shake my head. "If that was going to happen, you would have done it already. Go see MD at the compound."

"Where are you going?"

"I need to blow out some cobwebs and clear my head."

Scout chuckles. "Thought your head would be well and truly blown."

I shoot him a piercing look. "It was like fucking a corpse. She's one twisted bitch."

"Nah, she just likes it rough."

"Next time you can do it."

Scout raises his eyebrows and looks back at the building. "You think there'll be a next time?"

Throwing a leg over my bike, I turn it on. She springs to life with a loud, thunderous growl. Scout gets on his and grins, his mind clearly on pussy. With a wave, I peel away from the warehouse, leaving it and Camilla Sanchez in the dust.

Chapter 2

VIVIAN

"Book a holiday," they said. "It'll be fun," they said. Well, they didn't have to sit in economy from Brisbane, Australia, to Jacksonville, Florida. The cheapest, quickest flight I could find had a two-and-a-half-hour layover in Auckland, New Zealand, and another layover in Houston. It's taken me twenty-four hours, but I'm here.

Reaching up, I open the overhead locker and pull out my cute, leopard-print carry-on with gold zippers. My former friend, Jade, suggested I buy it. My friend who slept with my boyfriend. Shaking my head at the unpleasant memory, I smile at Ria, the little old lady sitting next to me. She boarded in Houston and has been a chatterbox for the last two hours and fifteen minutes.

The joys of being of a flight for hours means I

smell like the ass end of a bull. Ria didn't seem to mind though. She told me she's here to visit her granddaughter in Jacksonville.

"Would you mind getting my bag?" she asks.

Looking at the man behind me, he shuffles back a little so I can pull the bag down and let Ria out of her seat. Awkwardly, I tie my sweater around my waist, drape the coat I was wearing when I left Australia over my arm, and sling my ugly anti-theft handbag across my body. It was another suggestion from Jade. She said if I was ever going to travel, I'd need it. But I used to travel all the time and never needed anything so ugly. Thinking back, Jade must have planned to steal Todd all along. She always showed me travel brochures for exotic places. Maybe she hoped I'd get killed in the Congo or something.

"Thank you." She smiles widely as she gets to her feet with a groan. "These old bones don't travel as well as they used to."

"Tell me about it. I need a hot shower and sleep."

Ria reaches out and touches my arm. "Don't sleep yet. It's early. Wait until tonight. You're young, pretty, and on holiday. Go find yourself a hot young man to spend some time with."

I glance at the man behind me, and he flashes me a creepy grin. Now I wish I hadn't shared quite so much with her.

"No more men." I arch an eyebrow at him and

look back at Ria. "I might become a lesbian."

Ria bursts out laughing. "What happens in Florida stays in Florida."

Looking forward, I'm relieved to see the other passengers are slowly making their way to the exit. "Yay. We're moving!"

Ria picks up her bag and holds it in front of her. "I think this is the worst part, waiting to get off the plane."

"Yeah, that and going through customs. Oh, and waiting for your bag to come through to baggage claim."

Ria nods. "Yes, it can take forever."

"Well, I just hope my bag made it here."

"That's right, you came from Australia, didn't you?"

"Uh-huh. Hopefully, it's waiting for me."

Ria shuffles forward as we slowly walk toward freedom and the terminal. "Does it get hot in Australia?"

"Yes, ma'am! It gets up to forty-two where I'm from."

"Only forty-two?"

Realizing she's talking Fahrenheit and not Celsius, I say, "Hmm, it's about one hundred and seven for you."

"Oh my! Well, you're going to love it here in Florida. It gets to about one hundred and twenty," she teases.

Ria has no idea how much I'm going to enjoy this place. I live in a small country town, and it's winter in Australia. Apart from my cheating ex and my slutty best friend, the cold was another reason to escape. It gets down to minus ten. I've been wanting to move for the longest time, but with Todd and Jade living in the same town, I thought I had a home. Turns out it was all a lie. They deserve each other, and I deserve better.

The flight attendant smiles broadly at me as I deplane.

"Vivian, where are you staying?"

Looking down at the older woman, I realize she's been trying to keep up with me and is puffing hard. I stop walking and reach for her bag.

"Let me carry this for you. I'm at the Four Points. It's right on the beach."

"Oh, I'm fine." Ria swats at my hands but allows me to help her anyway. "That sounds nice."

Shaking my head, I keep walking at a slower pace toward the baggage collection area. "It's no trouble. Besides, we're going to the same place."

She smiles. "You know, my suitcase is the same as your bag." She motions toward my carry-on.

"I got a matching suitcase. We're twinning!"

Ria laughs. "I adore leopard print, don't you?"

Thinking about it, I grin. "Hells yes. It was hard to find something with gold zips. Most suitcases either have boring plastic ones or silver ones, but I wanted gold."

"Me too."

When we get to the carousel for the bags, the people from the plane are all crowded around it.

"Why do they do that?" asks Ria.

"I have no freaking idea. If they'd stand back, they'd be able to see when their bags are coming and get them easily. Instead, like sheep, they all mob together and no one can get their bags. You know, I watched mine go around three times once but couldn't get to it."

"Have you traveled a lot?"

"A little. Before the world imploded with COVID, I used to go to the UK every year."

Ria looks up at me. "Why did you decide to come to the States?"

"I needed a change of scenery after you know what. I've never been to the States, and Florida is supposed to be warm, so I'm living it up in the sun and surf. Even in summer in the UK it doesn't often go above thirty."

Ria frowns at me and appears to be confused.

"Sorry, eighty."

"Ah, right."

My bag appears on the carousel, and I wink at Ria. "Wish me luck. I'm going in."

Pushing my way through the throng of people, I get to the carousel in time to grab my bag. Being the nice person I am, I return to my spot next to Ria.

"My bag is coming around now."

Turning around, I see a leopard-print suitcase, the same as mine, and I dance through the waiting passengers and pull it off the belt. When I get back to Ria, she hugs me.

"Thank you!"

"You are more than welcome, but don't get too close. I must smell awful."

Ria wrinkles her nose. "You're fine."

Chuckling, I hand over her bag. "Sure." I place my carry-on over the handle of my suitcase and pull in Ria for a quick hug. "Thank you for making the flight from Houston a delight."

Ria laughs and shakes her head. "I'm not sure I made it a delight, but it sure was nice chatting with you."

Smiling at the older woman, I make my way out into the warm Florida air. I find the taxi queue and stand at the end of it. In the distance, I can see Ria getting into a black SUV with tinted windows that block anyone from seeing inside. It looks expensive.

"Ma'am, where to?"

I look up at the gentlemen with an expectant look on his face. "I'm going to Jacksonville Beach."

"I can give you a good rate." He moves to grab my things, but I nudge them further away from him.

"No, thank you. I'm good waiting for a taxi."

"I'll give you better rates."

Not knowing who this man is, I shake my head.

"I'm good."

"Come on, give a guy a break. I'll do it for fifty." He again tries to take my bags.

"I said no."

"Buddy, you heard the lady, move along."

Turning slightly, I see a policeman giving my would-be driver a meaningful scowl.

"We're cool, we're cool. I was only trying to save her some money." The man backs away, and I smile at the policeman.

"Thank you."

"You were right to say no. Never get into a car with someone you don't know. Book an Uber, a Lyft, or a taxi, but never someone like that. There are plenty of places to dump a body in Jacksonville."

Raising my eyebrows, I nod. "Good to know."

I didn't do a lot of research on Florida before I came. The thought of winding up in a ditch somewhere is a sobering thought. How well do you really know anyone? Hell, he could have been a serial killer.

The officer nods at me and continues walking. Looking around, I take in my surroundings. I've traveled a little, and I've never felt unsafe in any of the cities I've been to. My philosophy is, if someone feels dodgy, they probably are, and I should be wary of them. It doesn't matter if I'm in London, Florida, or my hometown. It's important to always be vigilant. People can get taken advantage of anywhere.

A taxi pulls up in front of me, and the driver pops the trunk and gets out to load my suitcases. "Where to?"

"The Four Points at Jacksonville Beach."

"Oh, fancy." He winks at me and opens the passenger door. "Love the accent."

I climb in, and he shuts the door and gets into the driver's seat. "And I don't have an accent, you do," I tease.

He laughs like he hasn't heard that one before and smiles at me in the rearview mirror. "You don't say? Where are you from?"

"Australia."

"You know, I've never been. What's it like?"

"Right now, it's winter, and it's cold."

"Ah, lucky for you, Florida is always warm, even in winter."

"Sounds like my kind of place."

The drive from the airport takes about forty minutes. My driver is in his sixties and chats the entire way. Sitting in the back of his cab, I feel myself drifting. Sleep is calling my name, and I know I need to stay awake, but my body is having none of it. The car comes to a halt, and my eyes fly open.

"Hey, Aussie, we're here."

"I must have fallen asleep."

"Oh yeah, you snored."

Bugging my eyes out at him, he bursts out laughing. "That'll be sixty-three dollars and seventy-nine cents."

Chewing on my bottom lip, I fumble in my handbag for my wallet. "Does that include your tip?"

"Ah, you Aussies don't tip, do you?"

"No, sir. If you don't mind me asking, how much should I give you?"

"The standard is 20 percent. More if you like the service, less if you don't."

Not being completely awake, I hand over eighty dollars. "Is this okay?"

He grins. "Do you want change?"

Tipping is completely alien to me. We don't do it in Australia, and they don't do it in the UK either. Not wanting to offend him, I shake my head.

"You can keep it."

"Aussie, I like your style."

He gets out, opens the trunk, and pulls out my suitcases. Gratefully, I take them off him.

"Thank you, Mr.?"

"Tony. Everyone calls me Tony." He reaches into his top pocket and hands me a card. "You need a lift anywhere, you give me a call, Aussie."

I slip it into my ugly handbag and do up the zip. "Thank you, I will."

Tony climbs back into the cab and drives away. Breathing deeply, I suck in the warm sea air and make my way through the doors of the hotel. I picked this hotel because it's right on the beach and has a bar, a restaurant, and a pier. For the days I don't want to do any sightseeing, everything is at my fingertips without having to leave.

As I walk to the concierge desk, the woman behind it smiles at me. "Welcome to the Four Points by Sheraton. How may I help you?"

"G'day, my name is Vivian Lewis. I'm booked in here for the next six weeks."

"Ah yes, Miss Lewis, we've been expecting you."

I'm sure they have. For the amount I'm paying to stay here, I could buy a very nice car back home. My mother sold her property and moved closer to the coast, giving me a share of the profits. Truthfully, I should have invested it in something or purchased a home of my own, but I had to get away. This trip is expensive, but I threw caution to the wind and booked it impulsively.

Opening my purse, I pull out my passport and my credit card and hand it over. "I've got an oceanfront room, yes?"

The woman beams at me. "We upgraded you to an executive suite. Not only do you have an ocean view, but you also have a living room to spread out in, and we've put you on our highest floor."

My mouth drops open. "You didn't have to do that."

"You booked and paid for six weeks. We want

you to be comfortable."

She looks past me, and I turn to see who or what she's looking at. There's a man there, and he's walking toward us.

"This is Jimmy. He'll escort you to your room and take your luggage."

"That's not necessary–"

She holds up a hand to stop me. "It's our pleasure. I'm Fiona. If you need anything, please don't hesitate to call me."

Jimmy takes my bags and wheels them toward the elevators. Fiona holds out a small folder.

"Inside, you'll find two room access cards and some information on tours in the area. Enjoy your stay, Miss Lewis."

"Vivian. Please call me Vivian."

Fiona smiles at me, and I take the folder. Jimmy holds the elevator door open for me, and I walk quickly to join him inside. He hits the button for the top floor, and we ride the elevator in silence.

The whole time I'm trying to figure out how much to tip him. Is a dollar an insult? Is five dollars, okay? Feeling completely out of my depth, I glance at him.

"Uh, Jimmy?"

"Yes, ma'am?"

"How much do you normally get tipped for taking someone's luggage to their room?"

"You're Australian?"

"Yep."

"The standard is a flat five dollars plus a dollar for each bag. If you're happy with my service, you can, of course, tip more." He smiles and walks ahead of me down the hallway to my room.

Right. Seven dollars. If I'm happy, I can tip more. So is that ten dollars?

Jimmy stops walking and looks at me. "Your key?"

"Right, right!" The cards spill out onto the floor as soon as I open the folder. "Shit!" Bending quickly, I pick them up and hand one to Jimmy. "Sorry."

He laughs. "No need to apologize." He opens the door, walks in, and holds it open for me.

All I can see is the ocean behind him, and I walk toward it. This room is enormous, and the view is spectacular.

"This is your living room." Turning, he nods toward a doorway and walks through it. I quickly follow him. "Here is your bedroom, and through that door," he points, "is your bathroom."

My eyes instantly go to the large windows in the bedroom and the view of the ocean. Being from a small country town, I don't get to the beach very often.

Jimmy clears his throat. "Would you like me to open the champagne?"

Turning, he gestures toward a bottle in an ice bucket next to a fruit platter on the coffee table in the living room.

Shaking my head, I say, "No, thank you. I think I'll leave that for later."

Jimmy nods and looks at me expectantly. It's then I realize I need to tip him. Opening my handbag, I search for a ten-dollar bill. All the bills in Australia are different colors so they are easy to find, I've got five hundred dollars in US currency. Well, I *had* that much before I paid for the taxi. All US money looks the same, and it takes me a minute to find the ten.

"Here you go. Thank you."

Jimmy raises his eyebrows and grins. "No, thank *you*. If you need anything, make sure you ask for Jimmy."

With a slight bow, he leaves me alone in my suite. Grinning to myself at the extravagance, I pluck a grape off the platter and put it in my mouth. Next, I make sure the door to my room is locked by sliding the bar lock. All I want now is a shower.

Placing my small carry-on bag on the bed, I open it and pull out the small pouch of toiletries and head for the bathroom. It's beautifully decorated in all white and has a shower over a small bathtub. When I turn on the water, it immediately comes out of the bathtub spout, so I push the button and it spurts out of the shower head. As the water heats, I eagerly strip off my clothes, put toothpaste on my toothbrush and then stand under the spray, nearly scalding myself. It takes me a little time to get the right temperature, but when I do, I clean my teeth and let the water wash over me.

There's no greater feeling than being clean after such a long time without a shower. The hotel has provided little bottles full of expensive shampoo, conditioner, and shower gel, and I use all of them. When I'm finished, I smell like a peach.

Smiling to myself, I towel down and walk back into the bedroom. I should really unpack, but the bed is calling my name. I grab another towel, lay it over the pillow, and crawl under the covers. Having kept the curtains open, I stare out at the ocean and finally relax. Within moments, I'm fast asleep.

Chapter 3

CAMILLA

Ria is one of the oldest mules we have and has never messed up a shipment—until today. She's sitting in a chair, her eyes filled with tears and wringing her hands as we stare at the suitcase full of clothes, not my drugs.

"I swear, it's simply a misunderstanding. Her name was Vivian. She must have gotten her bag mixed up with mine."

"So there are *two* of you with tacky taste in luggage?"

"Y-yes?"

Drawing in a deep breath, I scowl at Ria. "Why didn't you check the tags?"

"I assumed Vivian did. She's staying at the Four Points at Jacksonville Beach."

"Ria, I want to believe you–"

"Camilla, I would never betray you! Your family has been good to me."

Tilting my head to the side, I raise an eyebrow. "You told my father this was your last run. Did you decide to make some extra money on the side?" Her face pales. "How could you be so stupid?"

"No, no, no, I would never betray Señor Sanchez!"

"Hmm."

"Or you! Your family has been good to me."

Looking past Ria, I lock eyes with one of my men. He opens his jacket, showing me his gun. Screwing my face into a frown, I try to decide what to do with the woman. This is a way for Creed to make up for the lost bricks and prove himself to me.

"You said she was at the Four Points?"

"Yes!"

"And her name was Vivian?" Ria nods quickly and repeatedly as she fidgets in her seat. "I'll send someone to retrieve what's ours. But if you've betrayed me, Ria, it's not just you who will pay the price." Ria stands, and I shake my head. "Until we get back what is ours, you'll be my guest."

Her features twist into fear, but she nods. "Yes, Camilla."

Turning away from her, I stride from the room and pull my cell phone out of my pocket. Creed's number is stored under "RB" for Royal Bastards MC. Smiling to myself, I hit the call button. It rings for what seems like forever and then his voice greets me, but it's only a voice message. Frustrated, I hang up. If he's busy doing something, he might not realize it's me calling. After our little fling the other day, he might be avoiding me.

Mentally, I shake myself. It was the best fuck I've had in a while, so surely, he enjoyed himself too? The thought of him makes my heart beat a little faster and my blood burn with desire. He's everything I thought he would be in a lover. Forceful, domineering, and made me come so hard I could have screamed.

I'm a little disappointed he hasn't contacted me since our encounter. Most men fall over themselves to be by my side. But not Creed. He's never so much as looked in my direction. He's always about the business deal. Part of me believes it's because of my father. He would not be pleased that I've been intimate with a biker. Father wants me to marry a rival cartel's son to unite both families. But the man is insipid. He's never done a day's work in his life and isn't involved in the family business. There are even rumors he's gay. My suggestion was for Gabriel to marry their eldest daughter, but Father doesn't like that idea. He wants his only son to find his own path. Being a woman, it's never been that easy for me. I've had to prove myself every step of the way. No man ever gave me anything, but I've taken plenty from many. With my father's begrudging approval, I've turned our drug business into a thriving enterprise, something I don't think Gabriel could have done. He might want to take over what I've built, but it will always be mine, and I'll never let him forget it.

Drawing in a deep breath, I hit the call button for Creed once more.

"What?" His tone takes me by surprise.

"Creed?"

"What do you want, Camilla?" There's no affection or softness to his voice.

"I have a way you can make things up to me."

"Not interested."

A snarl escapes me. I might want to have him in my bed, but no man disrespects me … ever. "Not even if it means you won't have to lose the 2k?"

"Fuck," he mutters. "What do you need? And this isn't me saying I'll do it."

His insolence angers me. "One of our shipments has gone missing. I need you to personally retrieve it for me and dispose of any inconveniences."

A bitter laugh filters down the line. "So, you've lost another shipment?"

"Not me. My courier had it taken from her. Hopefully, it's simply a matter of a mixed-up bag, but it could be something more. Either way, I want it dealt with and my product returned to me."

"This isn't something I want to talk about over the phone."

This man infuriates me. I've tried to be as tactful as I can over an open line without saying "Get me my drugs back and kill the woman." It's not like I haven't done this a thousand times before.

"I'll send Hector to meet you at the warehouse. He can fill you in."

"Which warehouse?"

"The one with the broken window. The one you broke." I hang up on him and smile.

My body wants to meet him there so badly, but I won't let a man control me. Creed will learn I'm a woman who always gets what she wants.

Chapter

CREED

It's nearly eleven as I make my way into the warehouse. Hector is waiting in the shadows near the entrance. The only reason I know he's there, is the cigarette I can see burning in the darkness.

"Creed." He steps out of the shadows. He's dressed in a black suit with a black t-shirt. Hector always looks like he's stepped out of the pages of a magazine.

"Hector."

He tosses the cigarette to the ground and extinguishes its amber light with his shoe. "She's young, blond, Australian. Vivian Lewis is her name. She's staying at the Four Points."

"We have a connection there."

"Good. The mule believes it was a simple mix up, but who doesn't check the tags on their baggage?

Kill her, but not before we get our product back."

"And if she doesn't have your goods?"

Hector's lips purse together, and he puts his hands in his pockets. "Well, that won't bode well for you. Camilla won't be happy, no matter what you say or *do*. She specifically asked for you to look after this, so don't let her down."

Word has obviously spread I fucked their leader. My only response is to give him a chin lift. Turning, I walk back to my bike and ride toward town. It's a nice night and there won't be a lot of traffic on the streets. It takes me less than an hour to get to the hotel, and I park a few blocks away.

Taking my cellphone out of my pocket, I dial Fingers, our computer hacker.

"Hey, Creed."

"Fingers, I need you to work your magic and tell me everything you can about a woman staying at the Four Points. Her name is Vivian Lewis."

Before I finish talking, I can hear him tapping on his keyboard.

"Vivian Lewis. She's staying at the Four Points for six weeks." He whistles. "Must have money. She's booked into a suite with an ocean view, and it must be costing her more than ten grand to stay there that long."

Hector's mule might be wrong. Maybe her bag got taken on purpose, but then why tell her so much about herself?

"Thanks. Keep looking into her. If you find anything good, let me know."

"Will do."

I end the call and put my cut into my saddlebags before making the short walk to the hotel. Strolling into the lobby, I head for the bar. The bartender is the brother of one of my men. He nods at me as I sit. Without me having to ask, he pours a whiskey and slides the glass in front of me.

"Thanks."

"Can I help you with anything else?"

"Vivian Lewis checked in today."

He raises his eyebrows. "And?"

"I'll be needing a key to her room."

He stares at me for a good ten seconds then nods and walks away. He knows if he doesn't help me, it will look bad for his brother. Everyone and everything has a price. If he helps me, I'll help his brother which, in turn, helps their family.

While I wait for him, I look around the room. There are lots of vacationers but no drug dealers or police. No one pays me much attention. This is something a lower member of my MC would normally do, but as Hector pointed out, Camilla demanded I be the one to retrieve her goods and do the dirty work.

The bartender slides a keycard to me without making eye contact, and I slip it into my leather jacket. Draining the whiskey, I stand and walk toward the elevators. There's no one in the lobby, and the person at the front desk pays me no attention as I hit the button for the top floor. When the door opens, I step out into the garishly carpeted hallway. With little noise, I walk to her door and open it as quietly as I can. It doesn't open all the way due to the bar lock. This isn't something I haven't had to overcome before. I came prepared with a piece of string in my back pocket. Keeping the door open with my foot, I manipulate it around the bolt. Within thirty seconds I'm inside the room. Quietly, I close the door and allow my eyes to adjust to the dark. This Vivian Lewis has left the curtains pulled back, so filtered light makes it easy for me to walk around. Even the bedroom door is open.

My boots make little noise on the carpeted floors as I walk around the bed. She's fast asleep on her side. The sheet has fallen around her waist, exposing cream-colored skin. Vivian Lewis is beautiful—almost angelic—with her hands tucked underneath her head and her long blond hair swept off her face and across the pillow.

The suitcase, a tacky thing in leopard print, is in the middle of the room, seemingly untouched. Vivian sighs and wriggles on the bed. A snore escapes her, but she doesn't wake.

Apart from the ugly-looking luggage, she doesn't look like a drug dealer, but what does a drug dealer look like? From what Hector told me, their mule is an old lady. If I saw Camilla on the street, I'd think wealthy heiress, not a cold-hearted bitch who lusts for blood and power.

Moving to the suitcase, I pick it up and carry it into the living room. The lock on it breaks easily, and I unzip it. I find an assortment of clothes and nine statues of the Madonna, which I know are all filled with heroin. Closing the case, I carefully place it near the door. Camilla gave me explicit instructions. She wants this woman dead, but if she were a drug dealer, the case would have been hidden or, at the very least, she would have removed the heroin.

Standing over Vivian, I watch as a small smile spreads across her face and she sighs. I wonder what she's dreaming about. Perhaps I should end her life now, while she's in the throes of a nice dream.

But there's something about the woman— something in her smile. With a groan, I stare up at the ceiling. It doesn't sit right with me to kill her.

Shit.

Am I getting soft?

First, I fuck Camilla, and now I can't follow through with her bidding.

And maybe that's the issue. I don't like being told what to do, especially by her and the cartel. I've fought hard to be the president of my chapter. I've killed whomever I've needed to and done more deals with the devil to ensure I'm kept in power.

I don't answer to Camilla.

Vivian shivers and snuggles down further on the bed. Without thinking, I reach out and pull the sheet up over her.

"Thank you," she murmurs.

It comes out almost like a sigh, and I freeze. She doesn't stir or move. I hover over her for a moment longer, holding my breath, listening to her even breathing. Her face is slack with sleep. She's definitely not playing possum.

Tilting my head to the side, I study her features. Her plump lips appear to be a darker shade of pink, her nose is dotted with a dusting of freckles, and she has high cheekbones. If I'm guessing her age, she'd have to be twenty-four, maybe twenty-five. I wish she'd open her eyes so I can see what color they are, but having a biker leaning over her would probably fill them with terror.

Walking back to the door of her suite, I pick up the suitcase, open the door, and leave Vivian very much alive.

Screw Camilla.

When the elevator opens on the bottom floor, I walk out into the night and find my Harley. After strapping the bag to the back of my bike, I head for the clubhouse.

***

The compound is quiet when I pull into the parking lot. Taking the stairs two at a time, I enter the clubhouse and find my sergeant at arms, Winchester, sitting at a table. He has a bottle of whiskey in front of him and is staring at me with dead eyes. He wasn't happy I did this on my own. Winchester kicks out a chair opposite him, and it screeches loudly across the wooden floorboards.

"Winchester."

"Prez."

He licks his lips and pours me a drink. I sit in the offered chair, put the suitcase next to me, and lock eyes with him. Winchester is loyal to me, but he was also loyal to the last president. He respects power and authority but, like me, he didn't like the way the old president led the club. We have a code and have to make money, but he was taking us down a path to destruction. The old president got banished, and he's lucky I didn't kill him.

"How'd it go?"

I pat the bag next to me. "Smooth sailing."

"And the woman?"

My lips turn down in a frown as I nod. "Yep."

"Yep?"

I pick up the glass and swallow the contents, liking the burn as it travels down my throat. "Are you questioning me, Winchester?"

He takes in a quick breath, and his forehead creases as he raises his eyebrows in surprise.

Winchester leans back in his chair. "No, Prez. Just curious."

"It went fine."

"Where'd you leave the body?"

"In the hotel."

How do I explain I don't think she was involved? One look at her and I could tell she was innocent.

"What do you need me to do?"

I push the suitcase toward him. "Take this to the warehouse on the outskirts of town. There are nine Madonna statues inside. Make sure they all arrive safe and sound back to her highness."

Winchester smiles. "Rumor has it she's your new queen."

"Not fucking likely. I'd rather call you my bitch than deal with that cold piece of flesh." My top lip curls back in disgust.

Winchester holds up his hands and stands. "Sorry, Prez, it was something Scout said."

I should have known Scout couldn't keep his fucking mouth shut. The whole club probably thinks I'm with Camilla now.

With a shake of my head, I stand. "Yeah, I fucked it. Ain't going back for seconds."

Winchester grins. "I don't know, Prez, she looks all right to me."

"Then you and Scout can take turns for all the fuck I care."

He picks up the case and goes out into the night.

I look around the room at the usual half-naked club whores curled into a brother or simply lying on the lounge. No one else is awake. My mind goes back to the sleeping Vivian and how I can't leave her unprotected at the hotel.

Camilla wanted her dead, and if I don't do it, someone else will. Turning on my heel, I walk back to my bike and turn her on. No one comes out of the clubhouse. Retracing my path, I park in the same spot and remove my cut.

There's a homeless man asleep on the sidewalk. Apart from him and the odd drunken person, the streets are empty. The only sounds are the waves crashing on the beach.

As I walk through the lobby, there's no one at the desk, and I continue to the elevators. Again, I ride to the top floor and make my way down the carpeted hallway to her room. Using the keycard, I enter, but this time I go straight into her bedroom. She's still fast asleep. I make myself comfortable on the chair in the corner.

When Vivian wakes up, we need to have a conversation.

Is she innocent?

Or is she playing a deadly game with the wrong people?

Chapter 5

VIVIAN

Opening my eyes, I slide out of bed and peer out at the ocean as the sun slowly illuminates the world. Calm washes over me as I rest my forehead against the cool glass and watch the light reflect off the water. There are a few people down on the beach and from this distance they resemble ants. Being from a small country town, this view is breathtaking.

I'm not sure how long I stand and stare, but when my stomach rumbles, I know I need to get ready for my day and find food. Turning from the view with a sigh, I freeze. Slouched in the armchair in the corner is a man watching me through hooded lids. Slowly, he sits upright, his dark eyes never leaving me. I instinctively try to run, but he leaps across the bed and blocks the bedroom doorway.

"Don't scream. If I was going to harm you, I would have done it already." His voice is calm, as though he does this every day.

"W-What do you want?"

Fear overwhelms me as he points at the bed. "How about you put a towel around yourself, and we can talk?"

"If you come near me, I will scream. I will not go down without a fight. I have no fucking idea who you are, mister, but I am not some weak female you can have your way with." The words tumble out of my mouth, and I'm surprised at how sure of myself I sound.

He smiles and holds one hand to his chest and the other up in the air. "Again, if I was going to have my way with you, I would have done it already."

His eyes rake over my body. Tentatively, I take a step back toward the bed and reach for the towel. He doesn't move, and from the grin on his face he appears amused. Securing the towel around myself, I straighten my shoulders, raise my chin, and try to project a sense of calm as though this is a normal occurrence for me. Inside, I'm terrified as I try to figure out a way to get past him and out of the room.

"My name is–"

I shake my head vehemently. "I don't care! Don't tell me your name!"

He cocks his head to the side and puts his hands in the pockets of his jeans. "Vivian, you've seen my face. Knowing my name at this point isn't a big deal."

Aww, shit!

He's right. But how the fuck does he know my name?

Tears prick the backs of my eyelids as I realize I'm totally screwed. I'm in a country I know nothing about, and this man—this huge, muscle-bound man—is in my room. What the fuck am I supposed to do?

"Don't cry." His voice is soft, and he rubs the center of his chest with the heel of his hand, almost looking compassionate.

Almost.

"What do you want?" I whisper, scared he'll murder me, and my mum will never know what happened to me.

"There's a robe in your bathroom. Why don't you put it on? There's a coffee machine in the living room. I'll make us both a coffee and we can have a conversation."

Nodding, I walk toward the bathroom. Once inside, I can lock myself in. I reach for the robe hanging on a hook and attempt to shut the door, but he sticks out a boot-clad foot and stops me.

"Don't make this difficult, Vivian."

His eyes bore into mine, and I dip my chin in acceptance. Whoever he is, I can tell he's used to having people do as he wants. Keeping the towel on,

I wrap the robe around myself and tightly pull the ties together. He pushes open the door and gestures for me to walk ahead of him.

The living room furniture consists of a couch and two armchairs. The chairs look like the safest option for me, and I sit on the edge of one. He walks toward the door and slides the security bolt closed, then turns on the coffee machine.

"How did you get in?"

"Room key."

"But the door was bolted."

He chuckles. "Those things only keep out the good people."

Shit, shit, shit!

So he's not a good person?

"Are you going to hurt me?"

"How do you take your coffee?"

"Black."

"Me too." He says nothing more as he prepares our drinks.

Thoughts of my escape begin running through my mind. I could throw the hot coffee in his face and make a run for the door. I brace myself and try to muster the courage to carry out my plan.

He walks toward me and hands me the cup, but as I go to take it, he grasps it tightly.

"Don't do anything stupid, Vivian Lewis."

"I-I won't."

He holds it a moment longer, nods, and then

places his coffee on the table as he moves to the other armchair so he's facing me. I grab the cup and take a big sip.

"You've got pretty green eyes."

His comment surprises me, and I spit hot coffee across the room. He walks back to the machine and returns with a napkin.

"Sorry. Didn't mean to frighten you."

"Frighten me? You fucking terrify me."

He frowns, his lips turning down at the edges as he sits and leans forward, elbows on his knees.

"I'm Creed."

"Creed? What kind of name is Creed?"

"It was a name given to me by my brothers."

"What's your real name?"

He smirks and shakes his head. "Creed *is* my real name. The Royal Bastards are the only real family I've known."

"Why'd they call you Creed?"

He smiles, not a smirk, and his face lights up. He is good-looking in an I-can-take-care-of-myself kind of way. His t-shirt strains against his muscles, and the tattoos peeking out from under it make me wonder what they are. If he hadn't broken into my hotel room, I'd consider dating him. *Maybe* he's not so bad after all.

Creed steeples his ring-clad fingers together. "I have a set of beliefs that guide my actions. I don't waiver. If you fuck over me or my club, you're as good as dead."

Scratch that. This man is dangerous, and I'm trapped in a room with him.

"Are you going to hurt me?"

His hands fall to his sides, and he sits back in the chair. "Tell me how you came to get the suitcase."

"The suitcase?"

"Yeah, the leopard-print suitcase."

"My ex-best friend thought I should buy it. I liked it 'cause it had gold zips …"

As I speak, Creed's eyebrows come together as he frowns. "No, from the airport."

My eyes widen in confusion. "What do you mean? It came off the plane, went around the carousel in baggage, and I pulled it off. Then I came here."

Creed sighs. "You picked up the wrong bag."

Standing, I walk into the bedroom to prove the bag is mine. "No, I didn't."

I can't find the case, just my carry-on and ugly handbag. "Where is it?" I spin around, and Creed is right behind me. "Do you have it? It's got all my clothes in it."

Creed raises his hands above his head and leans on the door frame, his black t-shirt pulled tight across his chest.

"It's not here. It wasn't yours."

"Oh shit, did I take Ria's by mistake? We had the same bag."

He tilts his head to the side and stares at me as though I'm high on drugs or something.

"You're here because of a mix up? I would have returned the suitcase to Ria myself. There was no need to break into my room and scare the living daylights out of me. Jesus, you Americans are weird! All you had to do was ask!"

Still hanging on to the doorway, he laughs. His dark eyes lighten slightly as he watches me.

"You've no fucking idea what you've stumbled into, have you?"

"What do you mean?"

"Ria's suitcase was filled with heroin. You unwittingly screwed up a drug deal."

"Oh, my god. Is Ria okay?"

"You're worried about the mule?"

"She was a little old lady."

He lowers his hands and puts them on his hips. "Vivian, why do you think I'm here?" His voice is deadly serious.

"To get your bag back?" I whisper.

"Put yourself in my position. A stranger takes our product and checks into a fancy, expensive hotel. What would *you* think?"

I take a step back from him as fear crawls up my spine. "I'd think they'd stolen my drugs."

The light in his eyes fades as he nods.

This man means to kill me.

Licking my lips, I take another step back. Creed

tilts his head, and his mouth goes into a hard line. I move further away, and he shakes his head a little.

"Don't."

It's almost an order, but there's a hint of something else, as though he's begging me not to try anything. Sweat beads on my lip as fear takes hold. My leg muscles tighten as I turn and run for the bathroom and possible safety. Skidding on the tiles, I slam the door with all my strength, but it bounces off the door frame—or maybe off Creed—and flies open. He walks in, and a scream works its way up my throat.

"Don't," he warns again and clamps his hand over my mouth. "If I was going to hurt you, I would have done it already. Calm down."

He pins me against the bathroom wall with one hand over my mouth and the other on my waist, using his body to keep me in place.

"If you don't remain calm, I'm going to have to knock you out. I'd rather not do that."

Fear and adrenaline course through my veins. Thrashing about, I bite his hand and scream loudly.

"Fuck!" He reaches into his pocket and pulls out a sealed plastic bag with a white rag in it.

His weight leaves me as he opens the bag, and I manage to put some distance between us.

"Help!"

Creed shakes his head. "Remember, this is your fault."

"Fuck you! Help!"

He corners me once again and puts the rag over my mouth and nose. I breathe deeply and take in the sweet scent. Twisting my head from side to side does nothing to loosen his grip. Creed's eyes bore into mine as I try in vain to free myself. He's calm as I fight with everything I have. I kick, scream, and scratch, but he's an immovable object. My legs give out, and I know I'm about to lose consciousness. Staring him in the eyes, I try to tell him no, but he simply shakes his head.

"Sorry, Vivian. We'll talk when you ..."

Chapter 6

CREED

"Sorry, Vivian. We'll talk when you wake up."

With a grunt, I sweep her off her feet and lay her on the bed. Unlike the movies, it can take up to five minutes for someone to pass out using chloroform. I'm lucky it took her less than three. It was probably all the heavy breathing as she tried to escape. She's strong and has more than a fair amount of my DNA under her fingernails. The robe falls open, exposing creamy skin. Once again, I'm captivated by her but also a little ashamed. Quickly, I cover her up, pull my phone out of my pocket, and run a hand through my hair as I decide who I'm going to call. My vice president, Reaper, is the obvious choice. With a sigh, I tap his number and wait for him to answer.

"Hey, Creed, where you at?"

"I need a car. I'm at the Four Points."

"Kind of early for a pickup." Reaper chuckles. "You leaving the lady early? Wasn't she any good?"

"Reaper, park at the service entrance. Try to be discreet and call me when you're here."

Not waiting for a reply, I hang up and look down at Vivian. She's unconscious and should stay that way for at least twenty minutes. To be sure, I place the rag back over her mouth and nose. Counting to thirty, I pull it away and walk into her bathroom.

She hasn't unpacked very much, and it takes me less than a minute to put all her toiletries into a bag and her small carry-on. The leopard print strikes me as strange. She doesn't look like someone who'd go for animal print. She seems classier than that.

I place the carry-on on the bed, collect all her clothing, and zip it up. Going from room to room, I make sure she hasn't left out anything personal and then open the main door to her room. There's no one in the hallway.

I close the door and walk back into the bedroom to take my place in the armchair and wait for Reaper to call. My eyes travel back to Vivian, and I watch her chest rise and fall as she sleeps. Pulling out my phone again, I dial Scout.

"Yo, Prez."

"Scout, can you make sure I've got Advil in my room? It should be in the medicine cabinet in the bathroom. And put a couple of bottles of water by the bed."

"Sure. Something I should know? Reaper left in a hurry."

"All is good. Just do this for me, yeah?"

"Of course. You coming back to the compound soon?"

"As soon as Reaper comes to get me."

"Cool."

Ending the call, I take a deep breath and shove my phone into my pocket. This isn't going to go down well with the MC. I should have killed her. Standing, I stare down at her. Her hair isn't dyed, she doesn't have fake nails or a manicure, and her toenails look like she painted them herself. This isn't a woman trying to muscle in on a drug deal. A scowl settles on my face at the thought of hurting her because I'm pretty sure she simply picked the wrong bag off the carousel to help a little old lady.

What a fucking mess.

Camilla wants her dead.

I told Winchester she was dead. Well, not in as many words, but I implied she was dead. My phone rings, and I pull it out of my pocket.

"Yeah, Reaper."

"I'm downstairs. Do you need help?"

"No. Is there anyone around?"

"Nah, too early."

Tossing Vivian over my shoulder, I pick up her carry-on and her handbag and head for the main door to the suite. Opening it a crack, I peer out. No one is in the hallway. Swiftly, I walk to the elevator and hit the button. The hotel is quiet, but I focus hard to listen for any sound. If someone walks out of their room, I'm going to have a hard time explaining why I'm carrying a woman over my shoulder.

Thankfully, no one is in the elevator when it opens. I practically slam the button for the ground floor. It's a swift ride to the bottom. When the doors open, I wait a moment and slowly look both directions before getting out. Lady luck is on my side, there's no one around. I walk through a door with a "staff only" sign. From here, it's a brisk walk through the inner workings of the hotel to the service entrance. This early in the morning, so long as I keep away from the kitchens, I should be able to avoid running into any employees. A man walks out into the corridor. He has his head down and nods to himself as he plays with his phone. Without looking up, he turns around and walks in the same direction I'm going. Keeping my eyes glued to him, I continue down the hallway. He turns and walks through a doorway, and I pause to see where he went. A long corridor with four doors stretches out before me, but there's no one there. He must have slipped through another door. With a grunt, I readjust Vivian and open the door to the outside.

Reaper's eyes bulge when he sees me. "Prez?"

"Open the fucking door, Reaper."

He nods and runs to the Escalade. "You need any help?"

"No." Carefully, I lay Vivian across the back seat of the car and slam the door. "Keys?"

Reaper hands them to me. Reaching into my pocket, I hold out the keys to my bike.

"She's parked down the block toward the Crab Shack. You'll find her."

He lets out a whistle. "You want me to ride your bitch home?"

"Don't make it a big deal, Reaper."

"You got it."

He's in his late twenties, tall, and has a wiry body. No fat, all muscle. Reaper eats like a horse and never seems to gain a pound. He got his name from his morbid fascination with death. The man's head is shaved on both sides and long on top. It's braided and reaches his waist. We all have our issues, damaged in our own way, but Reaper is worse than broken. He's shattered.

He jogs away from me, and I climb into the car. I need to get Vivian away from prying eyes. The hotel has security cameras, but at this hour, I'm hoping no one saw us leave. Taking the back roads, I drive us into the Royal Bastards compound.

Winchester is waiting for me, hands on his hips and head tilted to one side. Sliding out of the car, I raise my hand and gesture for him to come over. With a frown, he drops his hands and lumbers toward me.

"Prez."

"Winchester." I toss him the keys to the Escalade. "Need you to move the car to the garage." Opening the door, I slide Vivian out and once again put her over my shoulder. "And bring the suitcase and handbag to my room when you're done."

"Didn't realize we were in the kidnapping business."

"We're not."

Striding away from him, I walk through the clubhouse and up the stairs to my room. The door is open, and I lay Vivian on the bed.

Scout walks in and smiles. "She's cute."

With a growl, I poke him in the chest. "No one is to touch her, understand?"

Scout holds up his hands. "It's all good, Prez. Who is she?"

"She's the fucking thief, isn't she?" Winchester enters the room with Vivian's things.

"I told you to move the car."

"*Fuck*," Winchester swears. "She's supposed to be dead."

Squaring up with him, I move into his space. "Move the fucking car."

Winchester steps back and nods. "I will."

"Good." He nods again. "Then get Reaper, he should arrive shortly on my bike. When he gets here, the four of us can discuss this," I gesture toward Vivian, "downstairs."

"You calling Church?"

"No, Scout, this is between the four of us."

Both men leave the room, and I cast a look at Vivian's sleeping form. She's still unconscious and should stay that way for a little while longer, but I know she's going to have a headache and feel nauseous when she wakes up.

Going into my bathroom, I open the medicine cabinet, grab the Advil, and put it on the bedside table. Scout has placed two bottles of water on my dresser, so I put them next to the pills. Opening my closet, I pull out a blanket and place it over Vivian. She's going to wake up scared in a strange place, so I might as well make sure she's comfortable.

Staring down at her, I whisper, "I'm sorry. Wrong place, wrong time."

She doesn't stir, not that I expected her to. I should have killed her, but it doesn't feel right. Shaking my head at my own failings, I walk out of the room, lock the door, and keep going until I end up in the room where my men await me.

None of them say anything. I position myself behind my chair at the head of the table stare firmly at the three of them. Scout squirms under my gaze, but Winchester meets my eyes without so much as a flinch.

I'm not going to sit. This shouldn't take long. They are with me or against me, and I don't keep traitors at my table. Make no mistake, this is *my* table. These men will bend to my will, or they'll be six feet under.

"What's the plan?" Reaper's dark eyes dart from Scout to Winchester and finally meet mine.

"She lives."

"You'll start a war over a woman?"

"Not over a woman, Winchester. We aren't lap dogs to the Diablo Cartel."

"No," he leans back and throws a hand in the air, "but we do work for them. They already think we're skimming. We should reassure them we have things under control, not disobey an order."

"I'm the only person in this room capable of giving an order to my club."

Winchester sucks in a breath, puffs out his cheeks, and lets it out slowly. "You know what I meant, Creed. Camilla thinks she controls us, and from what I hear, you're her new favorite fuck toy."

Slowly, I turn my head and pin Scout with a glare. The man shrugs and darts his eyes from Winchester to me.

"Didn't realize it was a secret," he mutters.

Gripping the back of the chair, I look up at the ceiling and twist my head from side to side, cracking bones and releasing some of the tension within me.

"The Diablo Cartel pays well, but they do *not* own us. She wants us to be exclusive, which means we'll have to give the Khans a definitive no and end up decreasing one of our streams of income."

Winchester steeples his hands together on the table. "Camilla said that? She said she doesn't want us working with the Khans?"

"Yes."

Reaper scrapes his chair back from the table and faces me. "I don't give a fuck who we work for, but why keep the woman alive? It'd be easier to kill her and dump the body in a swamp. What's the plan, Prez?"

"She's not a threat. Vivian picked–"

"Vivian?" Winchester's eyes widen.

"Yes, Vivian. She helped Camilla's mule at the airport. It was a simple misunderstanding. She's on vacation from Australia." I look at Scout. "Call Johnny. Have his brother, who works at the Four Points, check her out of the hotel and get her a refund."

"A refund?"

"Did I fucking stutter, Scout?"

"No, Prez," he says quickly. "But can I ask why?"

"We're going to make it look like she wasn't happy with the accommodations. She checked out early because of it. This way we can get a cut of the money and can keep an eye on her until it's time to put her on a plane and back down under."

"How is Camilla going to take the news?"

"Winchester, this club does *not* answer to

Camilla. And so long as you three keep your mouths shut, she will assume we put Vivian in the ground. It's an easy win for all of us."

Winchester nods. "Seems like a good plan. I've got no love for the Diablos, and I don't like Camilla telling us how we should run things. As long as we get a cut from Vivian, I'm down."

He says her name as though it's a stain on our existence. His tone grates on me, but I say nothing. My gaze goes to Reaper.

"Still don't know why we're keeping her alive, but I'm good." He smiles and stands. "If you change your mind, Prez, I'll put her down."

He means it. Reaper has never had a problem protecting the club. He'll do whatever it takes. Hell, he'd put his own mother in the ground if he thought she was a threat. All of us look at Scout.

"She's too cute to be made into swamp food. I'm happy to let her live." Scout taps his finger on the wooden surface of the table. "What are we going to do with her?"

Shit.

I have no fucking idea.

There's no way I can say that to these men. Killing is a necessity in our line of work, we've all done it. Scout is the softest of us. Murder doesn't sit well with him. He'll do it, but he likes to know why and if they deserve it. Reaper doesn't care. The man has ice in his veins. And Winchester? Well, he'll do whatever it takes to protect the Royal Bastards MC. We're the only family he's ever known.

I release a heavy sigh. "Leave that to me."

Winchester stands. "Sweet. I'm going to check in with the strip club, Prez."

"The one on Emerson?"

"No, the new one on Philips. The local cops have been giving us a hard time over health code violations, and I want to make sure the manager is handling them."

"Payoffs?"

His top lip curls. "Yeah, if that's what it takes."

"From that look, something's not sitting right. Need me to weigh in?"

"Nah. It's that cop, Schultz. He's greedy. I don't like men who renege on a deal. It turns my stomach."

"Killing cops is messy," says Reaper.

"We aren't going to kill a cop." I cross my arms over my chest.

Winchester shakes his head. "No, we aren't. Jesus, Reaper, don't you ever think things through?"

"We could make it look like an accident."

Winchester points at him. "Like that one you took care of in Gainesville?"

Reaper smiles as though he's reliving a good memory. "Yeah, why not?"

Standing straighter, I clear my throat as I walk toward the door. "Winchester, let me know how you get on. If he doesn't play ball, we'll find a way to make him play nice. Scout, get on the phone to Johnny. And Reaper, try not to kill anyone today." With my hand on the doorknob, I turn to face them. "Are we good?"

"Yep," Scout and Winchester reply in unison.

Reaper claps me on the back. "Let's go see if sleeping beauty is awake yet."

The last thing I need is Reaper anywhere near Vivian, but I have no good reason for him to stay away from her. Sure, I could issue him an order to fuck off, but it would be out of character, so I nod, and we walk back toward my room.

Opening the door, Reaper sidesteps me and walks in first. He's immediately hit over the head with the lamp that is normally next to my bed. He falls to his knees, and I put my arms around a screaming Vivian, frog marching her further into the room. Reaper stands, kicks the door shut, and laughs as he rubs the back of his head.

"Fuck! You broke the skin." His hand is covered in blood when he pulls it away.

With a grunt, I toss Vivian on the bed and point at her. "Enough."

"Fuck you!"

Reaper laughs louder.

I quirk an eyebrow at him. "What's so funny?"

Grinning, he nods at Vivian. "Been a long time since a woman, hell, anyone, has gotten the drop on me. This tiny little thing probably could have killed me."

"Come closer and I'll give it my best shot!"

Reaper doubles over, laughing. "I like her." He winks at me. "She's got spunk and fights like a ..." He shakes his head. "What was that cartoon creature from Australia who was like a whirlwind?"

"Tasmanian Devil," replies Vivian.

Reaper points at her and nods. "Yep, that's him, but you'd be a she-devil." His gaze comes back to me. "Devil. It's a good name for her."

Looking down at her, I raise a brow. Vivian is on her knees and wearing one of my black tees and an old pair of tracksuit pants with the legs rolled up to her knees.

"Nice outfit. Did you help yourself to anything else of mine?"

"You kidnapped me!" she hisses.

Reaper chuckles. "Got to give it to her, she's smart."

"Your sarcasm is duly noted." Vivian scrambles off the bed, putting it between us. "Are you going to kill me?"

"No. We've decided you aren't involved in the drug trade."

"Look who's smart now," Vivian retorts.

Reaper laughs loudly, and Vivian scowls and places her hands on her hips.

"This isn't funny."

He stops laughing, and the humor that once covered his face disappears and is replaced with the killer I know him to be.

Reaper takes two deliberate steps in her direction. Vivian, perhaps sensing the change in him, flattens herself against the wall.

"It's not funny. I'm VP here, and you assaulted me on club turf. I could kill you and no one would bat an eye. Do you have any idea how much trouble you're in?"

Her chest rises and falls rapidly as she looks at me.

He's right. He is within his rights to end her, and my chest burns at the thought. I give her a small shake of my head. Vivian's eyes grow wide, and she looks back at Reaper.

"You kidnapped me and drugged me. What did you expect me to do?" Vivian whispers.

Reaper grins. "You have a point, Devil." Reaper gives me a two fingered wave. "I'll leave you to it, Prez."

Staring at Vivian, I say nothing until Reaper closes the door. She's still against the wall, and a single tear falls down her cheek as she stares straight ahead. Moving slowly, I walk around the bed and enter her line of vision.

"Vivian Lewis, you need to calm down."

"Are you going to kill me?"

With my hands held up, I sit on the edge of my

bed. "No, we're not going to kill you."

She sighs and pushes herself off the wall. "Will you let me go?"

Tilting my head, I purse my lips into a thin line. "Can't."

"Can't. or won't?"

"You're going to be our guest. How long are you here for?"

"Why?"

I ignore her question. "You were checked into the Four Points for six weeks. Do you have reservations anywhere else?"

"N-No."

"Good. For the next six weeks, you'll be our guest."

"What?"

"We'll get you some new clothes and put a cot in here, so you'll be comfortable."

"But I'm staying at the Four Points."

"Not anymore, you're not. You'll be here."

"No, no, no!"

Vivian makes a run for the door. She pulls it open and is met with a grinning Reaper.

"Where you going, Devil?"

Vivian lets out a squeal and slams the door. With her arms wide, she leans against the door and slowly slides down to sit on the floor.

"This is not the holiday I wanted. I wanted a nice room, maybe a holiday fling, and to explore the town. Jesus, Jade is right. I'm a fucking fuckup. I probably couldn't get laid if I held up a sign."

"Who's Jade?"

Vivian's eyes land on me. "Aw shit, I was talking out loud again, wasn't I?"

"Yeah."

Pushing up with her legs, Vivian stands. "Just so I've got this right. You don't think I'm a drug dealer and you're not going to kill me?"

"That's right, and you're staying here until you fly home. Who's Jade?"

"I have tours booked."

"What type of tours? And who's Jade?"

Vivian puts her hand on her hip and cocks her head to the side. "Well, tomorrow I was going to hire a push-bike and visit some of the historical sites around Jacksonville."

"Push-bike?"

"Yes. Did you know Harriet Beecher Stowe, the author of *Uncle Tom's Cabin*, has a home that's still standing? It was built in 1871. It's one of many historical sites I want to visit."

Standing, I hold up a hand. "What's a push-bike?"

Vivian frowns. "It's a bicycle."

I smile. "Then why do you call it a push-bike?"

"A pushy is a bicycle. You use your feet to push it along, hence, a push-bike."

Putting my hands in my pockets, I chuckle. "And you think *we're* weird? I don't do bicycles.

Who's Jade?"

Vivian puts the heels of her hands to her eyes and rubs them. "She was my best friend until she slept with my boyfriend."

"Cunt."

She drops her hands to her sides and looks at me, a smile spreading across her face. "Pretty much." She giggles. "This is so much worse."

"Nah. I give you my word, you'll be safe here. And I'll make sure you get to see some of those historical sites, but not on a bicycle. I can arrange a bike of sorts." Winking at her, I move in closer, but she slides along the wall away from me. "Come on out and meet my men. I'll make sure you're treated like a princess. But Vivian, if you try to run, you'll spend the next six weeks in the hole. Trust me when I tell you, you won't like it."

I leave the door open when I exit and walk back downstairs toward the common area where we have a bar, our meeting room, and two pool tables. Highway, my road captain, is tending bar.

"Where's Sully?"

"She had stuff to do with her kid, so I said I'd cover her shift."

"Didn't know you two were so close."

"We're not, Prez, just doing her a favor. I like her kid. Stevie's good with anything mechanical."

"Is that the tall, skinny kid with the mohawk?"

Highway chuckles. "Yep. He can pull down a

motor and put it back together better than most." He pours me a glass of water and slides it across the bar. "One for the road?"

The boys know I don't drink before midday, but with the way my day's going, water isn't going to cut it.

Chapter

VIVIAN

My head is throbbing, I feel nauseous, my mouth is as dry as the Sahara, and I'm God knows where. This shit only happens in bad movies or cheesy romance novels. With a small push, I close the door.

I walk over and flop down on the bed and then look around the space. It looks like a college student's room. There's nothing personal apart from a framed photograph of a woman hidden underneath a box in his closet. Yeah, I went through his things. It's not like I was snooping, I was looking for a weapon. Don't all Americans have guns lying around? I read a book that said the ratio is something like five to every person, but I couldn't find one here.

Some Advil and two bottles of water are the only two things on the bedside table. The cute bastard must have known I was going to wake up feeling like crap.

Wait.

Did I just call him cute?

No.

He's not cute. He's brazen, cunning—a bastard. Although, he has nice eyes that light up when he smiles.

Growling at my thoughts, I take out two pills, open a bottle of water, and swallow them. The cool liquid feels great and eases some of the dry mouth I'm experiencing.

And who doesn't know what a push-bike is?

Every Australian kid has one, or they should. In my hometown, we have a program where underprivileged kids get a bike. We run a fundraiser each year to make sure it happens.

Looking down at my clothing, or Creed's clothing, I frown. I'm not even wearing a bra.

Ugh. Embarrassing.

A noise outside the door startles me out of my thoughts. Two, maybe three people are having a loud conversation in the hall. Wrapping my arms around myself, I stand and walk toward the chatter. With my hand on the doorknob, I steel myself and open the door. Two men and a woman stop arguing and fix their eyes on me.

The woman giggles. "Nice outfit."

Self-consciousness overwhelms me, and I pull

my shirt down, but then I remember I don't have a bra on and immediately release it.

The woman pushes past me and opens the door further to look inside. "Is Creed hiding in there?"

"N-No."

"No? Well, honey, where is he?"

Shrugging, I point my finger down the hall. "I think he went that way."

Giggling louder, she grins at me. "You coming?"

"I-I don't know."

She looks at the men. "How about you two rack up a table and I'll be there in a minute?" They simply walk away in silence. She waits until they are out of earshot before turning her attention back to me. "Are you okay?"

"No. Creed kidnap–"

She whips her hand up and places it over my mouth. "Oh, honey, I don't want to know. If Creed is involved, don't tell me."

Shocked, I raise my eyebrows, and she nods twice before removing her hand.

"Won't you help me?"

"Creed is king here ... or President." She titters. "I'm a club girl, no one's ol' lady. They call me Lucy."

"I'm Vivian."

"Nah, her name is Devil, Lucy. Make sure everyone knows." The guy I hit with the lamp walks past us holding a bag of peas to the back of his head.

Lucy moves closer to me, as though she's trying

to keep away from him. "Right. Devil it is."

He stops and looks at her. "You busy later?"

"Yep."

He looks her up and down, frowns, and keeps walking. "Pity."

Lucy links her arm with mine and leads me out of Creed's room. "You best keep away from Reaper. He's one damaged soul."

"Are you and him a thing?"

"Once upon a time."

Lucy smiles, but it doesn't hide an underlying sadness as she guides me downstairs and into a large open room with a couple of pool tables at one end. The two men from the hallway look at me as they chalk their cues.

Turning my head slightly, I take in my surroundings. An L-shaped bar lined with stools runs along one side. Tables and chairs scattered here and there take up a lot of the space, and a tattered couch that has seen better days is against another wall. A woman wearing short shorts is sweeping the wooden floors, her eyes glued to the back of a man sitting at the bar. She's focusing more on him than on her task. Behind the bar, a tall man with a beard, long hair, and a mustache grins at Lucy and me.

"Who'd you bring for us to play with, Lucy?"

The man sitting on the stool turns around. Creed.

"Nope, Devil isn't for playing with. Right, Creed?"

Creed shakes his head and stands, a glass of clear liquid in his hand. No doubt it's filled with vodka or moonshine.

Don't bikers make their own booze?

He takes a sip, and his lips turn down at the sides as though it tastes bad.

Yep, definitely moonshine.

"No, Devil is mine, and we're *all* going to leave her alone."

It's not like the room was bustling with noise, but at his declaration, we could hear a pin drop.

"I don't belong to anyone."

Creed grabs me by my upper arm and drags me to a table where he releases me and flops onto a chair. Looking around the room, I catch the eye of the bartender. He nods and begins wiping the bar top with a dish towel. I give Lucy a sideways glance as she sits on a stool. With no better option, I lower myself onto a chair opposite Creed.

"Would you like a drink?"

"Yes, but not what you're drinking. A soda, anything cold."

Creed looks at the glass and frowns. "Okay." He nods at the bartender. "Highway! Get Devil a Coke."

"Diet, please."

Creed chuckles and shakes his head. "Anything, but let's make it diet."

"I like diet."

Creed stares at me, takes a sip of his drink, and

smiles. "How are you feeling?"

"Like crap."

"Sorry."

Leaning forward, I hiss, "Are you?"

Creed sits back, stretches out his legs, and crosses them at the ankles. "I'm sorry you feel like crap. It's not a nice way to wake up."

"Someone has done it to you?"

He frowns and waves a hand in the air. "Tomorrow, when you're feeling better, I thought we might buy you some clothes."

"You're serious about not letting me leave?"

"Yeah. You have no idea about the things at play here." He holds up a hand as I open my mouth to speak. "No, I'm not going to explain it. The Royal Bastards are going to do our best to make sure you have a ... great six weeks."

"The Royal Bastards MC?"

"Yep."

"So, what, you're just going to chauffeur me around for six weeks?"

"Something like that."

Lucy places my Diet Coke in front of me. "Here you go, Devil."

Reaper walks into the room and starts singing the chorus to "Lucy in the Sky with Diamonds" by The Beatles.

Lucy groans and looks up at the ceiling. "I swear, Reaper, if you sing that fucking song to me one more time, I'll–"

He moves to stand next to her. "You'll what?"

Lucy steps away from him, shaking her head. "Try me and you'll find out."

"Lucy in–"

"Enough!" Creed roars. "For fuck's sake, Reaper, how old are you?"

Reaper looks down at Creed, clearly surprised at being called out. "I was only fucking with her."

"Yeah, well, leave it be."

Reaper looks at Lucy, then at me. "Cool. See you around, Devil."

He stalks out of the room, jogs down the outside stairs, and out of my line of sight.

"Sorry, Creed."

"Lucy, you can't talk to a brother like that."

"I know, and I'm sorry. He pushes my buttons and drives me crazy." Creed raises his eyebrows. "I know. I'll fix it."

Lucy leaves us and follows Reaper.

"What do you do here?"

Creed stands. "I'm the club president."

"Which means?"

"I'm in charge."

"Of what, exactly?"

Creed holds out his hand. "Come on, I'll take you on a tour."

Chapter 8

CREED

Devil looks at my hand in silence. For a moment, I don't think she's going to take it, but she does. She gasps at the same time a shock of electricity shoots up my arm.

"Static," I say, but she doesn't pull out of my grasp as she looks at our linked hands. With a slight tug, Devil rises from her chair, and I nod at Highway. "Our bartender is our road captain, Highway."

"Hey there, Devil. I'm guessing you're new to club life?"

She nods.

"Road Captain means I organize all the club runs. Make sure everyone has fun. I'm the guy you come to for a *good time*." He grins at her and winks.

Devil turns a shade of red at Highway's

double meaning.

Not liking the way he's looking at Devil, I scowl at Highway. He catches on quickly and chuckles.

Still holding her hand, I raise it and gesture to the back of the club. "Through those doors is the kitchen. Through that door is our meeting room." Gently, I drag her toward the hallway.

Missy, the club whore who's been sweeping the floors, clears her throat. Devil pulls her hand from mine and faces the other woman.

"Hello, I'm Vivian."

"No. Creed says you're Devil, so I'm calling you Devil."

"Right." Confusion settles on her face as Devil looks at me and scratches the side of her head before turning back to Missy. "And you are?"

"Not good enough by the looks of it," Missy sneers as she locks eyes with me.

"Devil, meet Missy." I reach out and grab Devil's hand again.

Missy stares at our connection and curls her top lip into a nasty smile. "Nice. To. Meet. You."

There's nothing friendly in her tone, and it's clear she doesn't approve of my interaction with the newcomer. Devil takes a step back and moves into my side. The warmth of her body against mine shoots another shock to my system.

I've never been with Missy. She's one of those club whores who's always looking for an old man, but she'll never be an ol' lady. The woman has one too many screws loose. One minute she's nice as pie, the next it's like she's flipped a switch. She's been warned: one more freak out and she's gone, dead to us.

Missy looks at our joined hands again and huffs before returning to her task with vigor. Devil looks at me, and I shrug. There's no trying to explain a woman like Missy to a woman like Devil. We all have our own brand of crazy. In fact, the way she's handling her incarceration is odd.

I turn and lead her down the hall where the patched members have rooms.

"These are all sleeping quarters for the highest-ranking members of my MC."

"And the stairwell at the end?"

"It leads upstairs to more bedrooms. Most of them are for the brothers who don't have a home of their own."

"Do you have a home of your own?"

"Yeah." Not wanting to explain, I nod back the way we came. "Do you want to see the kitchen?"

"Yes, I'm so hungry. I need some tucker."

"Is that meat?"

"What?"

"Tucker?"

Devil laughs and pulls her hand from mine to wave it in the air. "No, it means food."

"Tucker means food?"

"Yep."

"And you think us Americans are weird."

Devil walks ahead of me, avoiding Missy, and heads through the doors to the kitchen. Highway winks at me as we move through the room. When I enter the kitchen, Devil turns to face me with a large knife in her hand. I slowly move toward her with my hands in the air and lean against the island.

"Devil, I'd hate to hurt you … or worse."

The knife waivers in her hand, but I keep talking.

"I meant it when I said we'd keep you safe. I know this isn't the vacation you had in mind." I fold my arms over my chest. "Unfortunately, the woman who owns the bag you took … Well, she wants you dead. She thinks you took it on purpose."

"But I didn't. Can't you explain it to her?"

Shaking my head, I lock eyes with her. "She won't care. They kill people on a whim."

"And you don't?"

The corners of my mouth turn down in a frown. "No, I need a reason. A blind man could see you're an innocent in all of this."

The knife hits the kitchen bench with a *clang*, and a single tear runs down her face. "This was supposed to be the holiday where I reinvented myself." A sob escapes her, and she throws her arms in the air. "Jade and Todd are right. I'm useless. I can't even go on holiday without fucking it up!" Another sob bursts from her throat, and she wraps her arms around herself.

Something inside me hurts at seeing her so upset. Moving closer, I place my arms around her and stroke her hair.

"Jade, the ex-best friend, and I'm guessing Todd was the boyfriend?"

"Y-Yes."

"Fuck 'em. On my word, I promise you'll have a great vacation. If I can't take you where you want to go, one of the club women or one of the boys will. I'd only leave you with someone I trust. You'll do everything you want to do."

"Really?" Devil sniffles and looks up at me.

"But there are a few conditions. No running away, no more knives, and the club will want compensation for letting you stay here."

Devil pushes out of my arms. "What? You kidnap me and now you want me to pay you to stay here? *Here*?!" Her voice grows almost shrill, and she throws her arms wide. "Where there's not even a *pool*? Do you think I'm made of money?"

Scrubbing one hand across my face, I hold out the other for her to stop talking. "You're getting a refund from the hotel. All we want is five grand. You can keep the rest."

Her mouth drops open. "It cost me twenty thousand Australian dollars to stay in that hotel. That money was a gift from my mum. She could see how depressed I was. The hotel was beautiful, on the beach, and I could walk to a lot of places." A scowl flashes across her beautiful features. "I don't even know where I am!" Her voice rises. "Do *you* have a pool?"

Laughing, I shake my head. "No."

A fresh batch of tears wells up in her eyes. "I need to c-call my mum."

"How about we feed you first?"

Her bottom lip quivers.

"This way you can calm down. You don't want to worry her, do you?"

Devil turns her back to me and covers her face with her hands. "N-No." The poor woman releases another sob, and I have no idea how to comfort her.

Hell, if someone kidnapped me and asked for money to stay somewhere against my will, I'd kill them.

"How does a burger sound?"

"No, too messy."

Looking at her back, I shake my head. "Ahh, okay." I open the fridge to see what's available. "Grilled cheese?"

"Do you have tomato?"

I open the produce drawer, move some things around, and find what she's asked for. "Yes."

"Could I have a grilled cheese and tomato toastie?"

I don't really know what she means, but I'm gonna go with it. "Yep, I'm sure we can do that."

Snagging the tomato, cheese, and bread, I place them on the kitchen island.

Devil sniffles. "Want me to do it?"

"I've got it."

Moving around her, I pick up the knife she dropped, wipe it on a dish towel, and begin slicing the tomato.

"Don't you use a cutting board?"

"The island is made of stainless steel. I don't need a cutting board."

"Still, it's better for the blade. If you use a wooden or a plastic one, the blade won't chip or become blunt."

"We sharpen our knives. They'll be fine."

As soon as I unwrap the cheese slices, she frowns.

"What?"

"Don't you have real cheese? Not that processed crap."

"This *is* real cheese."

Devil groans and shakes her head. "No, it's not."

I open the fridge and move things around. The only other cheese I can think of is the canned stuff in the pantry.

"We have Easy Cheese."

"What the hell is *that*?"

My arm brushes her side as I pass her, and the electric shock courses through me again. Devil doesn't react, so I assume it's just me. Picking up the can, I shake it and hold it up to her.

"Easy Cheese."

"Oh my God, you can't eat cheese out of a can!" Her top lip curls as she recoils, but at least she's not crying.

I take the lid off and squeeze some straight into my mouth. "Mmm ... Tastes good."

Devil shakes her head. "I'll stick with the plastic-wrapped stuff. Where's the butter?"

"Why do you want butter?"

She shoots me a withering look. "To butter the bread."

"Why?"

She tilts her head and looks at me like I'm from another planet. "You don't make toasties very often, do you?"

"I've never made a toastie, but I make grilled cheese all the time."

"Where's the butter?"

"In the fridge."

Devil opens the refrigerator and searches for the butter.

"It's on the shelf in front of you."

"That's margarine."

"Yeah, butter."

Looking over her shoulder with her mouth open, Devil sighs. "You don't use *real* butter?"

"It's the same thing."

Pulling it out, she slams it on the kitchen island

and shakes her head. "No, it's not. Like your cheese, it's processed crap. Do you Americans know what's in your food?"

Holding up the can again, I spray more into my mouth. She looks at me for a moment, then butters her bread on both sides.

"Uh, why are you buttering both sides?"

Ignoring my question, Devil looks around the room. "Where's your sandwich maker?"

Not knowing what that is, I walk past her and pick up a cast-iron skillet and show it to her. Devil looks at me and then down at her sandwich.

"I guess that'll do. Could you heat it up for me, please?"

"Yep."

It's interesting watching her as she assembles her toastie. First, she puts on the tomato, then finds the salt and pepper, and finally she puts the "crap cheese" on top. Picking up her buttered monstrosity, she walks toward me.

"Where are your kitchen utensils?" She places her toastie in the middle of the skillet and looks at me.

"Most are hanging up over there." I point to the neat line of kitchen tools on the wall. "If you can't find what you're looking for, the big drawer over there will have it."

Devil moves around me, finds a spatula on the wall, and returns to her sandwich. "Did you want one?"

"No, I'm good. What did you have planned for your holiday?"

"The biking thing I told you about. There's a place called Pumpkin Hill Creek Reserve that has some really good hiking trails I'd like to try. And the beach, of course. I was going to spend a day, take a picnic, and just go for a walk."

"So you're really into hiking?"

"It's an inexpensive way to explore." She pauses for a moment. "Oh! And I was hoping to go to a college football game. Not that your football is as good as ours, but I'd still like to see a game."

I lift an eyebrow. "Why is yours better?"

Devil chuckles. "Your guys are all pussies who wear protective gear, and our guys are real men who don't."

Keeping a serious face, I say, "Sounds dangerous. At least our guys are looking after themselves and not taking unnecessary risks."

"Pfft! Pussies."

"Did you have anything else planned?"

"According to the internet, The Cummer Museum and Gardens are a sight to behold."

"A sight to behold?" I chuckle.

"Sorry, it's a direct quote from the website." Devil gives me a small smile.

"Wow. Okay, so you definitely had a plan."

Devil turns her toastie over and presses down on

it with the spatula. "Yeah. I live in a small town. If mum hadn't sold her house and gifted me some money, I might never have left it."

"So … you like living there?"

Her forehead creases, and her lips turn down at the corners. "Yes, and no. It was better when mum lived there and before the whole Todd and Jade thing."

"If it's one thing we admire here, it's loyalty and keeping your word. You shouldn't dwell on those two. They aren't worth the effort."

"You're right, but I had my life planned. I was going to marry Todd, and Jade was going to be my best buddy forever. When they did what they did, it gutted me. It was like someone had died except I got to see them most days, looking happy and living life." Devil's eyes meet mine. "They didn't seem to care that they'd destroyed me. They had each other, and I was left looking pathetic while they moved on. Even our friends chose sides. Jade and Todd ended up with the majority, and I was left with a few."

Moving closer, I raise my hand to touch her. When she doesn't' move away, I brush my knuckles along her jaw line. "Those are the ones you keep. The others are oxygen thieves and not worth your time."

Devil freezes at my touch, and I let my hand fall. She shrugs. "Still hurts."

Shuffling away from her so she feels safe, I say,

"Time heals all wounds."

Devil giggles. "Now you sound like my mum."

Highway throws open the kitchen door. "We've got company." His eyes stray to Devil.

"Diablo?"

"Yeah."

"Stay here with Devil, keep her safe."

"Is everything okay?" she asks.

"Yep. You eat your toastie in here with Highway. I'll be right back."

Highway jerks his head back in surprise, but he nods at me as I walk back through the clubhouse. Camilla stands near the tables at the front of the room, her face the very essence of disgust. As I walk toward her, she puts one hand on her hip and flicks her dark hair over her shoulder with the other.

"I thought there'd be more people here."

"What do you want, Camilla?"

"To talk."

"About what?"

She raises one of her perfectly arched brows. "We have a shipment coming in early. I was hoping you could handle it."

"When and where?"

Pouting, she moves closer and trails a finger from my chest to the top of my jeans. "Maybe we could talk about this in private?"

I quickly step away from her. "Not going to happen. It was a onetime thing. When and where are we meeting your shipment?"

An ugly sneer crosses her pretty face. "You think you're too good for me, biker?"

"It's not that. We're in business together. I don't want to confuse business with pleasure."

"You think I would do that?"

"It's not you, it's me."

"Pfft!" Camilla throws a hand in my face.

I grab it and move within an inch of her face. "Lady, I'm not fucking you again. Your father wouldn't like it, and neither would your brother. What we have here is a business arrangement, a *professional* arrangement, not a personal one."

Camilla licks her lips and smiles. "It could be fun?"

Releasing her, I step back. "When and where?"

Camilla scowls. "Hector!" One of her goons walks into the clubhouse. "Tell Creed everything he needs to know." Then she points at me. "The shipment better not be short."

Camilla looks me up and down, turns on her heel, and walks out of the building. I don't watch her go, but Hector does. When he can't see her anymore, he turns to face me.

"You fucked up."

"Already know that."

He nods. "She doesn't handle rejection well."

"Already know that too."

Hector cracks his fingers one at a time, stares at

me, then shrugs. "Tonight, at Stuart. It should be there at nine."

"That's a three-and-a-half-hour ride. Why are they coming in that way?"

"I'm assuming for I-95."

"Where are we supposed to check the shipment?"

Hector smirks. "Not my problem."

"I want it known, *Hector*, if we can't check it, it's on the Diablos, not us. I will not be responsible for something I can't physically count."

"Relax. There's a warehouse, it's secluded." He cocks his head to the side. "You can do *your* count." Hector turns and walks out of the clubhouse.

None of this feels right, and the way Camilla just acted makes the hairs on the back of my neck stand up. I feel like I'm about to be fucked over. Camilla is treating us like she owns us, but the Royal Bastards don't belong to anyone.

Chapter 9

DEVIL

Growing up, I never had a nickname, and Todd never called me "babe" or "love" or any kind of endearment. It's nice having people call me Devil, even though the name doesn't suit me. Unless they're being ironic. I'm the most straightlaced, by-the-book person anyone could ever meet.

Standing in the kitchen with Highway, I look around the room awkwardly, not knowing what to say.

"How long are you over here, Devil?"

"Six weeks. Do you have a pool here?"

He laughs. "No. But we could make you a redneck pool."

"Do I want to know?"

He laughs louder and shakes his head. "How do you know Creed?"

I'm a little puzzled at his question, but I guess not everyone knows I've been kidnapped. "Uh, you know. I've seen him around."

Highway tilts his head, and I have no idea why I just lied. I should ask him to help me, but I have a feeling he's loyal to Creed.

"Right. How long have you been here?"

"I got in yesterday."

"And you've seen him around?"

Not wanting to answer any more of his questions, I nod and take a bite of my toastie. "Mmm, this is good, even with plastic cheese."

Highway looks down at me. "Do I want to know?"

Before I can answer, Creed opens the door to the kitchen and walks in. Highway gives him a chin lift and heads for the door muttering, "Plastic cheese?"

Creed grins and looks at me. "Is she still complaining?"

"Sort of." Highway claps him on the back and leaves us alone.

"How are you feeling?"

I hold up my toastie. "Better."

"Good. You look tired."

"Must be jet lag. I could do with a nap."

"Nausea? Headache?"

Tilting my head from side to side, I mentally feel out my body. "Nah, just tired."

"We haven't moved a cot into my room yet, but

you could sleep in my bed."

The thought of sharing his bed sends a throb of passion through me, and I shake myself. He might be good-looking, but he's keeping me prisoner. For all I know, the story about the drug cartel might be an elaborate hoax to extort money from me. Although, I don't think it is.

He bends and searches my face. "You good?"

"Yes."

Creed steps back and puts his hands in his pockets. "I have to go out of town." His top lip curls in distaste. "Business."

"From the look you just gave me, it's not going to be fun."

His lips twist into a smile. "Never is."

"You going to kidnap someone else or murder someone?"

He raises a brow. "It's not in the plan, but you never know how things will turn out."

"Who's going to look after me?"

He rocks back on his heels and looks at the ceiling. "I'll ask Lucy and maybe Reaper."

"Not him." His eyes come back to me. "He scares me."

"You hit him over the head with a lamp, so he can't scare you that much."

"Please?" My tone is almost pleading.

"Fine. Let me see where Scout is." Devil smiles. "Come on, I'll escort you to your room."

"You mean *your* room."

Creed shakes his head and opens the door to the kitchen. A whole lot more of the MC members are milling about. Lucy is playing doubles on the pool table with Missy and two men.

Both men stare at me as I walk out. Highway is behind the bar, and I give him a small wave. One of the men at the pool table licks his lips and nudges the guy next to him. He scowls at him and turns his attention to Creed.

Creed lifts his chin at the man. "Justice, you got a minute?"

Justice shoots a scathing look at the man leering at me and walks toward Creed. "Always, Prez."

"Aww, we're one short with him going," Missy whines.

"Not a biggie. I can drop out." Lucy puts her cue back on the rack.

Missy stomps her foot. "Lucy, need you too."

Creed points toward his room, and I take the lead and walk ahead of them. When they all enter, I'm sitting in the middle of Creed's king-sized bed with my legs crossed.

"Lucy, Justice, this is Devil. She's our guest for the next few weeks." Creed looks at me, then back to Justice. "I'm out of town tonight with the Diablos. I need you to keep Devil here in the compound, safe and untouched."

"If you're doing a run, I should be with you."

"Not tonight." Justices opens his mouth, but Creed holds up a hand, silencing him. "I need you two to make sure Devil is looked after. Think of her as MC royalty."

Lucy's eyes bug out of her head and her mouth drops open. "As in an MC princess?"

Justice smirks. "Never thought I'd see the day."

"Don't read too much into it," Creed says, but Justice continues to stare at me. "Keep her safe."

Lucy sighs. "Why am I involved in this?"

"You're a woman, and she might need a woman's perspective."

Clearing my throat, I get the attention of all three of them. "I won't be any trouble. I'm going to have a nap now. Maybe later we could think about food?"

Justice stares at Creed. "How long are you going to be gone?"

"Unsure."

"Great." His gaze locks on me. "Devil, you do what I say when I say it. I'll be near the bar. After you've had your nap, come find me." Justice turns on his heel and leaves the room.

Lucy walks over to me. "Do you need anything?"

"Some underwear would be nice. Could we go shopping?"

Lucy looks over her shoulder. "Creed?"

"Give Lucy your measurements and she can get you something. If you're going out in public, I want to be by your side."

"I'll be fine."

"Yes, you will be. I'll make sure of it." He speaks as if it's an order.

Annoyed, I roll my eyes and smile at Lucy. "I only know them in Aussie sizes, so I should probably wait until I can try them on."

Lucy pulls her phone out of her pocket. "I can google it."

"Nah. I've ordered enough things over the internet to know I need to try them on." Thoughts of an evening dress I ordered filter through my mind. The website said it was a medium, but it must have been made for a small child, not a medium Aussie girl.

"I've been there," Lucy agrees.

Creed frowns. "Tomorrow, we'll do the bike thing and go shopping."

"You're going to take me on a push-bike?"

"No, but the next-best thing."

Lucy frowns. "Okay, well, I'll be with Justice near the bar." She turns her attention to Creed. "Maybe I could find her one of my tighter tank tops to wear so she doesn't feel so ... exposed?"

Peering down at my boobs, I totally understand what Lucy is saying. Although I'm not well endowed, I have enough that a bra would be appreciated. When I look up, Creed is staring at my chest. I self-consciously cross my arms over my chest.

He smiles. "If it will make her feel more comfortable, yes."

"Hey! I'm right here." I look up at Lucy. "Yes, please, I'd appreciate it."

"I think I have an older one with built-in bra support. It's not a bra, but it will strap you down a bit."

"Thank you."

Lucy winks at me and heads for the door, leaving Creed and me alone.

"You've got a nice rack, you shouldn't be embarrassed." Heat infuses my face, and although I know he's trying to give me a compliment, it feels very inappropriate from my captor. "You're blushing," Creed teases.

"Men don't normally comment on my chest."

"Yes, they do, but they probably don't let you hear."

Pursing my lips together, I stare at him, not knowing what to say. Do I say thank you? Or do I simply ignore the comment?

Creed walks to the end of the bed and puts his hands around the rail. His hands look rough, as though he does manual work.

"Do you have everything you need?"

"Apart from my freedom, you mean?"

Creed grins. "Come and lock the door."

Scrambling off the bed, I do as he says. Creed stands at the door. For a moment, I think he looks unsure, but a man like him probably does this kind of thing every day. He cups the side of my face with his hand and sweeps his thumb across my cheek, sending shivers through me.

"Keep the door locked while you're sleeping. No one should come in here as it's my room, but you don't want someone accidentally coming in and thinking you're available."

"That's a thing?"

"No, but I don't want anyone touching you."

His hand falls away, and I take a step back from him.

"Take care on the road. Do you know when you'll return?"

"Around two."

"In the morning?"

"Yeah." He chuckles. "You a morning person, Devil?"

"I'm a breakfast person."

Creed laughs louder. "I'll remember that."

His dark eyes appear lighter. It's nice to see a softer side. As though a switch has flipped, the light dies and they go back to being dark. "Lock the door."

Creed walks out into the hallway, and I shut the door and lock it. Someone, I assume Creed, jiggles the handle.

Is it strange I like that he's checking on me?

Or I like the touch of his hand on my face?

I know I shouldn't. He's my captor, after all, but I'm drawn to the man who wants to keep me safe.

Chapter 10

CREED

With Reaper and Scout with me, we mount up and head for Stuart. It's a nice day, the sun is shining, and the weather is warm. It'd be a nice ride if it wasn't for the fact I feel like a dog on a leash doing Camilla's bidding.

I should never have fucked her. Me doing this run is her way of keeping me in line. I'd bet my last dollar she organized this run just to see me and feel me out.

What a fucking mess.

Visions of Devil run through my head. Chuckling at the thought of her, her accent, and the strange things she says makes me wish this run was over.

Scout pulls up alongside me, points at his face, and grins manically. Scowling, I pull ahead of him, but he catches up and shakes his head at me. He's my closest friend in the MC. Scout is a patched-in member and my tail gunner, so me pulling ahead of him shouldn't upset him too much. As tail gunner, his position is always at the back of the pack. It's an important role. Scout protects us from behind, making sure we are protected when we have to turn or change lanes. He does it all first, making sure the cars slow down or stop completely and then the rest of the pack move over.

Although he is my friend, Scout likes to push my buttons better than anyone else in the MC, but he also always has my back. Sometimes he doesn't know when to shut his mouth, but he'd be one of the first to step in front of a bullet for me, not that he'd need to.

Reaper pulls alongside me, a bandanna pulled up over his mouth and dark glasses covering his eyes. There's a truck stop ahead, and he signals he wants to pull into it. I nod and hold my hand up, letting Scout know we're pulling off. We've only been on the road for an hour and should ride on through, but I'm in a good mood. If Reaper needs a break, I'm cool.

We pull in and park. Reaper is the first off his bike. He stretches and looks around, pulling down his bandanna as he does.

"Sorry, Creed, I needed a drink."

"You feeling okay?"

He rubs his arms. "Yeah. Fucking Lucy

apologized to me and it's messing with my psyche."

Scout does a double take then walks away from us quickly. Reaper doesn't do emotions.

"You like Lucy?"

His lips turn down, and he shakes his head. "Nah."

"You like Lucy," I repeat. It's a statement this time, not a question.

He pulls down his shades and looks at me over the top of them. "Does it matter? You know me. You know how I am. She deserves better."

"Yes, she does." This is new territory for him, and it's not a path I think he should go down. "Keep away from her. Be civil, be fucking polite, but I'm ordering you to keep away. Lucy is off limits."

Reaper nods. "I'm going to go get that drink."

"Is your head on straight?" He grunts and walks toward the truck stop. "Reaper, I need to hear you say it," I call out to his back.

He stops and I hear his intake of breath. "Yeah, I got it. Lucy is off limits." Reaper keeps walking.

From the way people are moving out of his way, he must we wearing his trademark scowl. Shaking my head, I follow him inside. Scout is flirting with the waitress behind the counter and, from the way she's blushing, she likes it.

Reaper stands next to him, and the smile on her face disappears as he says something to her. Scout waits until her back is turned before he gives

Reaper a scathing look and mutters to him. From here, I can't hear what it is, but Reaper simply grins and walks back to me.

Scout is two steps behind him. "You know, Prez, your VP can be a dick."

"Fuck you, Tail Gunner. Remember your place."

"What you just did had nothing to do with my role in the MC. You were striking out because you're too fucked up to close the deal with Lucy."

Reaper grabs Scout by his cut, and I make a noise in the back of my throat. Both men look at me, anger on their faces.

"Let. Him. Go." Reaper immediately does as I say and steps back. "Scout, go check your bike." The man nods at me, but not before his top lip curls up at Reaper. My hand goes to Reaper's chest. "Lock it down. You do *not* get to take out my decision on Scout."

"The man is a walking fuck stick."

I chuckle. "That may be true, but he's your brother. Don't be a dick."

He purses his lips and nods. "I'll buy him a soda."

"You'll fucking apologize."

He nods once and walks out. I snag three bottles of water and hand over some money to the cashier, who looks slightly flustered at having to serve me.

I grin. "You have a good day."

Picking up the bottles, I walk back toward the boys. They're shoving each other, but it's more playful, not aggressive. Scout smiles, and Reaper flips him the bird. When I'm close enough, I toss each of them a bottle.

"Take a sip and mount up. We've got a couple more hours to go."

My phone rings and it's Winchester.

"Yeah?"

"Creed, we've got a problem with Heelz and that cop Schultz."

Raising my eyes to the sky, I sigh. "He won't play ball?"

"Nah, he wants more green."

"Fucking greedy cunt."

"Yeah. What do you want to do?"

Scrubbing a hand over my face, I look down at the ground. "Set up a meet. Let's try and come to an agreement we can all abide by."

"Will do, Prez."

He ends the call, and I put my phone away.

"Problem?" Reaper takes a sip of his water as he climbs on his bike.

"Nothing that can't wait." I move toward my bike. "Let's get moving."

***

We drive straight through without any more stops, and the sun is setting when we arrive in Stuart. We're hours early, but I like to prepare, get a lay of the land, and make sure there's nothing out of the ordinary.

Reaper climbs off his bike and stretches. "Want me to do a walk around? See who's here?"

"Here" is an old warehouse on the outskirts of Stuart. There's no one around that I can see. But inside, I'm not sure.

"Yeah, check it out." I nod toward the building. "Take Scout with you."

The two men walk toward the warehouse. Scout shoves Reaper, and he shakes his head. Their squabble is clearly over. It's not easy managing the different personalities in an MC. Scout is the easiest to read. He rarely lets things bother him. But Reaper, he's led a life of hardship, far worse than mine.

His confession about Lucy was a surprise. Sure, I knew he liked her, but he's not one to want to settle down, nor should he. More than one of the club girls has called out for help while being in his room. When Reaper sleeps next to a woman, things happen. He's been known to nearly strangle them without even waking. One time, he pinned a girl to the bed with a knife to her throat.

Reaper is the man someone wants next to them in a fight, but he's not the man I'd want dating my sister. Lucy is new to the club. She's liked and hasn't turned into a whore. The scuttlebutt is she had a fling with Reaper, but ended it abruptly. Since then, she's steered clear of him and made herself useful around the clubhouse. Lucy is an awesome cook, and more than one brother has made a move, but she hasn't let anyone claim her so far, which means she's one hell of a strong woman.

Taking in my surroundings, I suddenly realize it's too quiet. I can't even hear the noise from I-95. Reaper and Scout emerge from the building, walking quickly and scanning the area. On instinct, my hand drifts to the gun in my holster. Reaper makes it to me first, and Scout turns, watching the warehouse.

"What is it, guys?"

Reaper's eyebrows are drawn together. "Dead body in the office. He's been tortured." He scrubs a hand over his face. "They cut off his dick, it's in his mouth."

"You see anyone around?"

"Nah. Doesn't look like anyone has been here for a while. The body is at least two days old."

"Fuck it. I knew it couldn't be easy. Fucking Camilla." Sighing, I scan the area again. "Let's move the bikes. I'll phone her majesty and see if this is one of her little games. It might be a setup." My hands fall to my sides. "Did either of you touch anything?"

Scout shakes his head but doesn't turn around. Our Tail Gunner is keeping watch.

"No, Prez, we weren't born yesterday. And I took

a photo of the guy." Reaper holds out his phone to me, showing the grotesque image.

"Good. Come on, let's stash the bikes."

***

"Well, if it isn't my favorite biker," Camilla purrs into the phone.

"Are you fucking with me, Camilla?"

"Well, I'd like to, but you're playing hard to get."

"Who's the dead guy?"

"What?"

"You heard me."

"Wait." Camilla puts me on hold.

"Did she know?" Reaper whispers.

"I'm thinking not."

The line clicks when Camilla returns. "Who is it?"

"Check your messages. I sent you a photo."

"Jesus, why didn't you simply paint a picture in the sky so everyone can see it?"

Again, she puts me on hold, and out of frustration, I punch the tree in front of me. Scout laughs and Reaper's brows shoot up nearly to his hairline.

"He's not one of ours. But we have had some issues bringing product in from that direction."

"Why the fuck didn't you tell me?"

"Because I thought it was resolved."

"It looks like your friend has been here for at

least two days.”

“I can’t divert the shipment. I’m sure whatever this is, you’ll handle it. Let me know when it’s done.”

“Don’t you dare hang–” She ends the call, and I once again punch the tree. “Fucking bitch.”

“What’d she say?” Reaper begins to pace.

“She told me dick. The only thing she said was they’d had issues and she can’t divert the shipment.”

“What are we going to do?” Scout runs a hand through his hair.

“Did you bring a rifle?”

Reaper stops pacing and looks at me. “Yeah.”

“Find high ground. Let me know if anything doesn’t look kosher. Scout, you find somewhere near the warehouse, but stay out of sight.”

“Where are you going to be?” Reaper’s forehead creases.

“I’m going to be visible when the truck pulls in. You two are going to have my back. If anything looks out of place, shoot everyone.”

Scout shakes his head. “I don’t like this. Let me be the one out in the open. You should be in the shadows. Besides, you’re a better shot than me.”

Reaper nods. “He’s right. You’re more important than him.”

“Fuck you, Reaper,” Scout replies, but he’s smiling.

The thought of one of my men getting killed in my place doesn't sit well with me. "It's not my first rodeo. I'll be fine."

"I'm sure the man in the office thought that too," Reaper counters.

"True."

Reaper is right, this whole thing feels wrong. My gut tells me we should cut and run. It's either a fucking setup or someone is trying to muscle in on the Diablos. Either way, we are in the middle of a shit storm. The Royal Bastards have protected the Diablos' shipments for a long time. It's not only their reputation on the line, but ours too. If I'd known this was going to be a cluster fuck, I would have brought more men.

Fucking Camilla.

"We've got hours before the shipment arrives. Reaper, find high ground. Scout, you and I are going to hide out of sight and see what unfolds."

"I like this plan better." Reaper walks to his bike and pulls a case out of his saddlebags. "This way, none of us are taking unnecessary risks."

"Aww, were you worried about me?" Scout bats his eyelashes.

"Nope."

Reaper walks away, and Scout grins at me. "You know, I think I'm growing on him."

"Nope!" Reaper shouts over his shoulder.

Shaking my head, I move into the trees to wait

and see if trouble comes looking for us.

***

The shipment is an hour late. No one has arrived at the warehouse, and I'm done waiting. Scout used to be in the Army, and it taught him to sleep when he can, so he's dozing on the ground beside me. The man can fall asleep in about five seconds flat.

Suddenly, he bolts upright and looks around frantically. "Are they here?"

"No. It's ten o'clock."

"It's late?"

"Either that or it's just not coming."

Scout stands and brushes himself off. "I don't like this, Creed."

"Me either. This whole excursion feels off."

"Yeah."

Headlights pierce the night air, and a truck slowly drives down the dirt road. Neither of us moves. The driver stops the truck in the lot, climbs out, and walks into the warehouse.

"Hello?" he yells after turning on the light.

"What do you want to do?" Scout whispers.

"He's alone."

Scout shakes his head. "He *appears* to be alone."

"I'm going in. See if you can get closer. Use the truck as cover."

"It's not the usual truck. This one has a container

on the trailer. They normally use a refrigeration truck. Creed, I don't like this."

He's right. We use refrigeration trucks for a couple of reasons. First, we can hide containers of product in all sorts of places. Second, if the truck gets pulled over, the people searching them don't normally spend too much time inside because of the cold.

I sigh loudly. "I'm going in."

Scout frowns but does as he's told, keeping to the shadows as he approaches the truck. Going in the opposite direction, I make some noise to get the trucker's attention.

He turns and raises a hand. "Are you the guy I'm handing over the truck to?"

The man appears to be in his late sixties. He's smiling and has on a red tattered baseball cap.

"No, I'm supposed to escort the truck."

He shakes his head. "No, that's not how this works. I ain't driving the cargo any farther. My instructions were to meet Charlie. He's supposed to pay me, and then someone takes the truck the rest of the distance. It's been nearly a day since I began my trip. I'm done, son. It's all yours as soon as I get my money."

"I've done this before. We don't take possession. We count the product, we escort and guard, that's all."

"You want to count 'em?" He tugs on his ear as

though he's confused.

"Yeah, to make sure the shipment isn't short."

"No one's ever counted 'em before." He takes off his cap and rubs between his eyes. "Son, they've been in there a day. It's pretty disgusting by now."

Confused, I walk closer to the man. "What do you mean?"

Scout comes out from his hiding spot. "There's people in the container."

The old guy's eyes grow wide with alarm, and he backs up when he sees Scout. "Where's Charlie?" He turns slightly. "Is he in the office?"

"Give me the keys so I can open the container."

He puts his cap back on and looks from me to Scout. "You're not here for the container, are you?"

Scout looks at me. "How long have they been in there?"

"He says the better part of a day."

"In this heat?"

"Charlie normally looks after everything. Is he here?"

"What's your name?"

He holds out his hand. "Luke."

Ignoring his hand, I nod toward the warehouse. "Luke, there's a man in the office. He's got dark hair, looks to be about thirty. Does that sound like Charlie?"

Luke scratches his head. "Yeah. Should I get him from the office?" He takes a step toward the warehouse, but Scout moves to block him.

"Luke, give me the keys to the container." The man reaches into his pocket and pulls them out. "Don't go into the office."

Taking the keys off Luke, Scout and I walk toward the back of the container with Scout and climb onto the truck's platform. Using the keys, I undo the padlock and pull on the chain securing the door and let them both fall to the ground. Grabbing the handle of the container, I pull it up and throw the door wide. The first thing to hit me is the odor.

Excrement.

Sweat.

Fear.

Death.

Scout gags, moving away from the havoc before us. The few who are alive look almost dead. Holding my arm over my mouth to block the stench, I move into the container filled with mostly women and a few teenage boys. There's a bucket in the corner overflowing with human waste. A woman at my feet reaches for my boot and I swoop down and pick her up.

Scout holds out his arms and takes her from me. "Jesus," he whispers as he carefully lays her on the ground. "Are there more?"

Words fail me, so I nod and walk back into the container of death. I check the pulse of a small boy near the entrance, even though his eyes stare blankly ahead. He can't be more than thirteen. Next to him is a girl. They look similar, so I'm guessing she's a sister or close relative. She has her head on his shoulder. Moving her long, dark hair, I hold two fingers to her throat and feel for what I hope is life. She murmurs something, so I pick her up and carry her out. A few others open their eyes, silently begging to be let out of this hell hole. One by one, I pick them up and hand them off to Scout. Before long, Reaper joins us. He climbs into the back of the container, and we carry the living out to Scout.

"You've gotta understand, it's a job. I've only had them for not even a day." Luke looks down at the bodies with fear and revulsion on his face. "I didn't know."

Scout grabs him. "Why wasn't there a fan or a way to cool them down?"

"There was! But I went through a blockade, so I turned it off. I-I forgot to turn it back on."

Reaching down, I pick up the hand of a small girl and her skin peels off. It must be from the heat. It's as though she's been cooked. Gagging, I stand and back out of the container. There are still so many bodies lying inside.

"It's okay, Creed. Go help Scout. I'll check them all, but I think the rest are dead."

Jumping down, I move away from everyone and suck in the clean night air, trying desperately to keep myself from vomiting. After a few moments, I turn and walk toward Luke.

He did this.

He let those people die.

The man looks at my face, shuffles backward, and he runs toward the warehouse. For an older man, he's fairly quick, but he's no match for me as I chase after him. My hand lands on his shoulder as he throws open the office door and sees his friend.

The color drains from his face, and the tendons in his neck stand out as he turns to me with wide eyes.

"Please don't kill me!"

"We didn't do that. We don't do *this*!" I point at the handful of survivors outside the container. "Who do you work for?"

"You know!"

Grabbing the man, I drag him toward his truck and the people on the ground. "How long were they without air and water?"

Luke shakes his head and wrings his hands. "I forgot! I've done this a dozen times and nothing like this has ever happened before!"

Pushing him closer to the people desperately trying to cling to life, I take a deep breath as my hands clench and unclench in barely contained rage. "Have you ever checked before?"

His eyes meet mine, and he stops shaking his head. "N-no."

"Creed! We need water or we're going to lose all

of them." Reaper's voice is filled with urgency. With his fists hanging at his sides, he locks eyes with me and then turns to Luke, with a murderous glare.

"Luke, is there water here?"

"There's a bathroom through the office."

"Do you have anything in your truck to get the water to them?"

"Y-Yeah in the truck." Luke moves to the driver's side door and climbs in. He throws out six plastic drink bottles and a large container with a spigot on it.

"Go fill these up. Don't touch anything in the office."

"I-I can't go back in there."

Roughly, I shove him toward the survivors. "You'll do it and you'll do it now or, by God, I'll put a bullet in you myself."

With his eyes glued to the ground, Luke picks up the plastic bottles, holding them in his grubby t-shirt so he can carry all of them. I pick up the large container and follow him to the office. Carefully, he walks around the body and goes into the bathroom. When I hear running water, I put the container down and go outside with Reaper and Scout.

"What the fuck is this?" Reaper's eyes are wide, and his nostrils flare as he barely controls his anger.

"No fucking idea."

"We don't run people, Creed."

Sure, we own strip clubs and brothels, but

everyone is there of their own free will.

Could we do more to help them out of the game? Probably.

But I'm not a saint.

I stare hard at the weakened people lying on the ground. "No, we don't."

Luke comes out of the office, his t-shirt wet on the front as he carries the bottles tied up in it. Reaper and I walk toward him and take the six plastic bottles.

"I left the container just inside the door," Luke offers, slightly out of breath.

I'm sure seeing his friend all cut up is tough on him, but I don't want to risk my DNA or my men's DNA ending up in someone's lab. We've all done time, and we aren't going back.

Reaper kneels next to one woman, and Scout puts his hand on his shoulder. "She's gone."

He says nothing as he moves to the next. I throw Scout a bottle, and he holds it to the lips of one boy.

There are twelve people on the ground, over twenty dead in the container, and I have no fucking idea why we are here. Holding a bottle to an older woman's lips, I slowly let the water trickle into her mouth. She looks at me wildly with sunken eyes as she tries to swallow. The temps are cooler tonight, but it's Florida, so not exactly cold.

She raises a hand to hold the bottle.

"You got this?" I whisper.

She gives me nothing in the way of recognition, so I say, "Lo tienes?"

My Spanish is rusty, but I know a few words. She nods. I release the bottle and move on to the person next to her.

Luke comes lumbering out with the large container, clearly struggling to hold it. "I filled it all the way."

"Luke, could you see if there is anything in the office or bathroom we could use?" I call out.

"I looked. There's nothing."

"Buckets?"

He shakes his head but stops and thinks for a second. "Wastepaper bin?"

"Anything that will hold water, go get it," Reaper growls.

I sigh. "Reaper, they need a hospital."

"They're illegal."

"They're going to die if we don't do something."

"We could call MD?" Scout suggests.

"He's at least three hours away." I look around at our bleak situation. "Suggestions?"

"Miami's chapter is closest and Tampa isn't far either." Reaper suggests.

"I don't want to get another chapter involved."

"We have a relationship with Hatch in Miami and Ominous in Tampa. They were both in Waterton with Bounty."

Hatch is a straight talker and, like most of us, the

club always comes first. Then there's Ominous, Bounty speaks well of him and I know if I put the call out, he'd either be here himself or he'd send someone to help. But if I phone either of them, I'm putting us all at risk.

I'd be happier if Bounty was with us, but unfortunately, he still has time to serve on his sentence. He's one of my best men. Bounty is the guy we go to if we want someone, or something found. He's like a bloodhound. He also has friends in every corner of Florida.

Luke bends down and gives one boy some water.

"Luke, who do you work for?"

"Diablo," he answers flatly.

Fucking Camilla.

Is this why she didn't want us to check the shipments?

Has she been running illegals across the border instead of drugs?

"Burn it all, the warehouse, the truck, everything. We'll carry them farther away and call the fire department and ambulance."

Reaper's head snaps in my direction. "This is a bad idea."

"They're all going to die. Do you have a better suggestion?"

"Let me call Hatch or Ominous. They might help."

Scout keeps his mouth shut, his eyes glued to the people on the ground.

"Hatch is closer, I'll call him." Pulling my cellphone out of my pocket, I search for his number and initiate the call.

"Yeah?"

"Hatch, it's Creed. I need your help."

"Talk to me."

Moving away from everyone for some privacy, I begin to explain our predicament. "We had a run for the Diablos, but it wasn't what we thought. Turns out it's live cargo, or … nearly live."

"Illegals?"

"Yeah."

"How bad?"

"They've been in a container with no air and little water for the better part of a day."

"More dead than alive, then?"

"Yeah. Hatch, it's a fuckup. The few who are alive aren't going to make it unless we get them help."

"Where are you?"

"An old warehouse off I-95 on the outskirts of Stuart."

Muffled voices filter down the line, but the words are indistinguishable. Finally, after what feels like forever, Hatch comes back to me.

"We have a friend in Stuart. Send me the address, they'll be with you soon."

"How soon?"

"Half an hour or less. He's a wiry fucker with a bad attitude, but he's good in a medical crisis. His name is Preston."

"Preston?"

"Yeah. The man is a surgeon, but he's not right in the head."

"He gets the job done?"

"Yeah, we don't use him often. He works at a small hospital in Stuart. He used to be a cardiac surgeon until he wasn't."

"I owe you."

Hatch laughs. "Yes, you do. We'll be in touch."

He ends the call, and I text him the address. Hatch runs the Miami chapter of the Royal Bastards about a five-hour drive from Jacksonville. He's loyal to the club, so owing him a favor isn't so bad.

Scout stands next to me. "The boy is gone."

"Hatch is sending a guy named Preston. He should be here within the hour."

He nods and walks away from me and into the darkness. The boy must have touched something within him. There's nothing I can say to ease his pain.

"Scout, don't wander too far. You're needed."

Walking back to the bodies, I try to assess the damage. Reaper is dragging away two of them, which means only nine remain alive.

"Where's Luke?"

Reaper looks around. "Fuck. Sorry, Creed. I was preoccupied."

Walking back into the warehouse, I find him on

the telephone. As soon as he sees me, he hangs up.

"Who were you talking to?"

"No one."

Not wanting to waste time fucking around, I pull my gun from my holster, point it at him momentarily, then let my hand rest against the outside of my thigh. The man stares at me with fear in his eyes. My instinct is to shoot him and be done with the whole fucking mess. Luke's eyes drop to the floor, and he fidgets with his baseball cap. I'm not known for patience, but sometimes saying and doing nothing can be more terrifying than yelling or torture. Eventually, Luke's gaze comes back to me.

"Who?"

"Hector."

"And who does Hector answer to?" I tap the side of my leg with the gun.

"Gabriel."

"Sanchez?"

Sweat beads on his forehead and slowly travels down his temples and cheeks. It falls onto his dirty t-shirt when he nods.

"How often do you do this run?"

"At least once a month."

"Do you always come here?"

His eyes go to Charlie in the chair. His lips turn down at the corners and he pales. "I have a wife, children, grandchildren ..." Luke looks at me. "It's only a job."

"Yeah, I get it. They're not really people, they're product, right?"

His face flushes as a pained look crosses his features. "I don't ask. They pay well. I've got a family."

"Luke, I'm going to let you live, but only if you answer this question truthfully. Do you always deliver to this location?"

He nods. "I've never had a problem before. Charlie handles everything."

A loud whistle pierces the air.

"Fuck!" I hiss and run out of the warehouse.

"Incoming!" Scout shouts. "Three sets of headlights are coming down the road."

There's no time to hide the living and little time for us to get a better vantage point. Reaper has already disappeared into the shadows, and I hope he's got his rifle.

"Scout, go around the side of the building. I'll whistle if it's clear."

For once, he doesn't argue and disappears into the night.

Luke moves toward me. "What should I do?"

"Keep your mouth shut."

He freezes.

My gun is still in my hand, so I put it back in its holster and walk to stand in front of the people on the ground. Three vans pull up with tinted windows, making it impossible to see inside. The driver's door to the first van opens, and a man with an Uzi walks toward me. The hairs on the back of my neck stand up. Somehow, I don't think a cardiac surgeon would have an Uzi, even one who does work for an MC.

The man strides past me, looking at the people on the ground. "Where's Luke?"

Luke comes out of hiding and waves at the man, his face once again a mask of joviality. He clearly knows this man, and thinks he's safe now. He takes his time walking to us. The guy with the Uzi glances at me, then back at Luke.

Luke pushes his baseball cap up at the front, puts his hands in his pockets, and laughs. "I thought you'd never get here."

"What happened?"

"Border patrol stopped me, so I turned the fan off." He looks down at the people on the ground. "Forgot to turn it back on."

The man looks at me, then back at Luke, raises the Uzi, and shoots him several times. Luke's body twists around as though it's on strings. With a yelp, he falls to the ground, motionless. He then aims his gun at the remaining survivors. As he pulls the trigger, I knock his arm upward, and the bullets spray into the night sky.

More men pour out of the vans, and I hold my arms up. "I've got help coming for them."

"They're nearly dead. Useless to us."

"Give them a chance. Surely, Gabriel would like to recoup some of his money."

The man bends his neck from side to side, the bones cracking loudly in the night. "How far away are they?"

As if on cue, a car drives down the road and pulls into the lot. If it's Preston, he's not alone. There's a woman seated next to him. He says something to her and gets out of the car, arms raised.

"I'm Preston. Hatch sent me."

He's Asian, can't be over five feet tall, and has a long scar down his cheek. Slowly, he steps toward us, his gaze never leaving our new friend with the Uzi. When he's only about three feet away, a look of disgust crosses his face, and he quickly moves around us to the people on the ground.

"Jane! I need the saline and IVs, stat!"

Jane gets out of the car, opens the back passenger door, picks up two bags, and jogs toward us.

Preston moves from patient to patient, no longer paying us any attention. "Jane, they all need an IV. Do we have enough?"

"I think so." She opens one bag and tosses Preston an IV fluid bag.

Methodically, they go from patient to patient, and I'm left standing between two of the people holding up the fluid bags.

"Can your men help?" Preston asks the Uzi man.

He holds up an IV bag toward him, but he stares at him as though he's an ant he wants to squash. Uzi man remains silent but raises his head at his men who either holster their weapons or sling them across their bodies.

When Preston and Jane finish administering the fluids, he looks at me. "How could you have let this happen? These are people, not cattle. Hell, we treat cattle better than this!"

I raise my hands, palms out. "It wasn't me."

Uzi man chuckles and shrugs. "Wasn't me either. Dead cargo doesn't earn us anything. I'm simply the cleanup guy. How long before we can move them?"

Preston looks inside the container. From this level, we can only see the outline of bodies, nothing more. "Are there more inside?"

I shake my head. "All dead."

"You're sure?"

"Yep."

Uzi man taps Preston on the shoulder with the barrel of his gun. "How long before we can move them?"

"They need to be in a hospital."

Uzi man once again cracks his neck. "How long?"

"They have severe dehydration. It'll be two to three days of care."

Uzi man looks around as if he's bored. "We don't have that long."

"How much time can you give us?"

He holds up a hand, moves away from us, and pulls out a phone.

"Tell Gabriel I want to talk to him," I say.

Uzi man says something into the phone, grins and raises his eyebrows at me, then holds out the phone to me and waves it in the air.

Jane takes my position, holding the bags as I take the phone.

"Gabriel."

"Creed, they are of no use to me. My man there is dead, and Juan said Luke is too."

"You need to give them time."

Laughter filters down the line. "You will let Juan move them now, or he's going to put a bullet in every one of them."

"Including me?"

"You don't work for me. You work for Camilla. I see no reason for you to die, but the doctor and his pretty nurse? They are collateral damage."

"No."

"No?"

"If you bring shipments through here on a regular basis, they could be useful to you. Killing them would be a mistake."

Gabriel sighs. "You have a point. Can the cargo be moved now?"

"What's your hurry?"

"We didn't kill Charlie. A rival has done that. Who knows when they will be back? Either we move them now or we clean up. You decide."

The line goes dead, and I toss the phone to Juan. "Load them up."

"What? You can't!" Preston says.

Putting a hand in the middle of his chest, I lock eyes with him. "They're going to kill them if we don't let them load up now."

"They'll die."

"And so will we if we don't get them into those vans."

Preston and Jane share a long look before she nods. He puts his hands on his hips, and a growl escapes him. "Fucking bikers."

"Hey, man, this has nothing to do with us. I shouldn't even be here."

"Yet you are." Preston clears his throat. "You need to keep them on the saline drips. They need fluids but also electrolytes."

A man holding up two bags clears his throat. "Like Gatorade?"

"Yes, if you aren't going to take them to a hospital."

In the end, only nine people can be moved into the backs of the vans. The rest are either dead or too weak to move. Juan's gaze never leaves me. He stands over the bodies on the ground, looking down at them with contempt.

"Leave them to me," I snarl.

A smile creeps across his face and he shrugs. He

turns and, for a moment, I think he's going to leave them, but I should have known better. The sound of gunfire pierces the air as one of his men goes from person to person, snuffing out what little life they had left.

"No!" Preston yells, and I grab his arm, stopping him from interfering. "He's killing them!"

"Better them than us," I whisper.

The man's eyes are wide, and he jumps with each gunshot. "I took an oath."

"These men have no morals. They could easily kill you, me, and your pretty little friend. We aren't out of the woods yet."

When the last body has been shot, Juan stands before us, the Uzi still in his hands. "Thank you for your help. Gabriel appreciates the assist." He tilts his head and looks at Preston. "We'll be in touch." Reaching into his pocket, he pulls out a wad of cash and tosses it at him. The money bounces off Preston's chest and onto the ground. "The Diablos say thank you, and we look forward to working with you again."

I clear my throat and Uzi looks at me. "Where were you taking them to?"

"Why?"

"Only curious."

He looks me up and down. "Tampa. We have ships which take them all over the country or anywhere they're needed."

He gives me another cursory look, then turns and walks back to the van. I stand there, holding my breath as I watch them drive away. When I can't see their taillights anymore, I exhale, relieved the Diablos didn't end my life tonight.

Reaper emerges from the darkness, giving Jane a fright. She squeals and moves to stand behind Preston.

"You okay, Prez?"

Looking down at the people on the ground, I groan. "I've had better fucking days."

Preston, with his arm around Jane, hurries to his car. When they have disappeared into the night, Scout reveals himself.

He slowly takes in the carnage surrounding us and looks at me with sorrowful eyes. "What now?"

"Burn it all."

Moving away from my men, I call Ominous.

"Hello?"

"Ominous, it's Creed from the Jacksonville Chapter."

"Hey man, I know who you are. What can I do you for?"

"Diablo's run illegals through Tampa. They called their man, Juan. I was hoping you could do some recon and find out something about him."

"It's not a lot to go on. Why do you care?"

With a sigh, I scrub a hand over my face. "I know, but he just killed a group of women and children on

Gabriel Sanchez's say so. I'd like him to pay."

There's a sudden intake of breath and he says, "I'm on it."

"Thank you."

"Don't thank me yet. I'll want something in return."

"Name it."

Ominous chuckles. "I'll let you know," he pauses. "Soon."

The line goes dead and for the second time tonight, I've promised to owe another chapter a favor.

***

The sun is coming up as we enter the Royal Bastards compound. A couple of the boys are standing over a smoking firepit, the flames long since gone. Getting off my bike, I head straight for my room and shower. The filth of the night feels like it's smothering me. Scout and Reaper disappear into their rooms. None of us have said a word. We'll go over this in a few hours and call Church to decide what the club is going to do. I'd like to kill Camilla, but that would mean a war.

The door to my room is locked, and I pull out my keys to open it. Devil is asleep in the middle of the bed in a fetal position. Taking off my cut, I hang it on the back of a chair in the corner. I remove the rest of my clothes, letting them fall to the floor. Naked, I walk into the bathroom and wash off the stench from the past few hours. There's a bottle of liquid soap which must belong to Devil. I squeeze it, and the scent of apples fills the air. Lathering myself up, I scrub from head to toe, hoping the highly fragranced soap will remove the smell of today and ease my mind.

Wrapping a towel around myself, I walk back into my bedroom. Devil is still fast asleep. There's no cot in this room. My mind and body are exhausted, and I need at least a few hours of sleep before Church happens. I need to have a clear mind for what's to come.

Looking down at her sleeping form, I decide I'm going to lie down on my bed. First, I sit on the bed, but she's in the middle of it, all curled in on herself. The only thing I can do is wrap my form around hers. Keeping my towel in place, and I pull up the sheet, so Devil is covered and lie down. My arm goes over her and she sighs.

"Thank you," she mumbles, just like the first time I saw her.

Devil's breathing is even, and her hand entwines with my mine. Closing my eyes, I fall asleep to her breaths and feel a sense of calm wash over me. She doesn't know it yet, but I'm keeping her.

Chapter 11

DEVIL

Waking up from a deep sleep, I feel content. No, more than that. Whole. I don't think I've ever slept this well. With my arms above my head, I stretch. My leg touches another body, and I realize I'm not alone in the bed. Suddenly, I'm not content. I jump out of bed and look down at Creed's sleeping form. With a small smile on his lips, he rolls over, stretches out, and snores. As quietly as I can, I pad into the bathroom and shut the door.

What am I supposed to do?

Staring at myself in the mirror with my hair sticking up, I look like a crazy person and decide a shower is in order. I turn on the shower and strip off while the water warms. Once it reaches an acceptable temperature, I stand under the spray. Picking up my shower gel, I squeeze the bottle and realize it's almost empty. With a face cloth, I do what I need to do to get clean and then I pick up my almost empty bottle, wrap a towel around myself, and walk back into the bedroom.

"Creed! I can't believe–"

Standing around the bed are five men: Highway, Justice, Reaper, and two I don't know. My mouth drops open. I throw the bottle at Creed and slam the bathroom door. Laughter erupts on the other side.

After a while, there's a light knock on the door. "Devil, you okay?"

"You used all my shower gel. Lucy got it for me." More laughter. "I like shower gel."

"I'll get you some more."

Opening the door a crack, I peer out, looking for Creed. He's standing there in only his jeans. "Promise?"

"I think I said I'd take you shopping today."

I open the door wider. "You did."

He holds out a black t-shirt to me. "It's not much, but it's something."

"But you're taking me shopping?"

Creed raises his hands. "I will, but there's something I need to do first." He scrubs a hand over his face and turns away from me.

Shutting the door, I pull the t-shirt over my head. It's big, but it covers me. When I reopen the door, I find Creed sitting on the end of the bed.

"What's wrong?"

"Club business."

"Meaning?"

"Meaning, I can't talk about it."

Sitting next to him, I say, "Is this a normal thing?" Creed frowns at me. "You know I'm not part of your world. You can talk to me. No one will know."

He hangs his head, then glances at me and nods. "I'm president of this MC. This means I can't always share the things that happen around me."

"Like keeping me prisoner to save my life when it would be easier for you to kill me?"

Creed chuckles. "Yeah."

He twists to look at me, and I tilt my head to the side, waiting for him to speak.

He laughs again, but there's no humor in it. "We had a run last night. We were supposed to collect a shipment, count it, and escort it back." Creed inhales and slowly lets out the breath, flaring his nostrils.

"It didn't go to plan?"

"No." He looks up at the ceiling. "Instead of it being ... product ..." Creed's voice trails off.

"I'm going to guess product means drugs." He nods. "Keep going."

"It was people." Creed's face twists as though he's in pain. "It was a container full of people. Most were dead. We saved, well, I *think* we saved a handful."

"You don't know?"

"No. They were taken."

"Let me see if I've got this right. You were supposed to do a drug run, but the run turned out to be people, most of whom were dead. How come you thought it was a drug run?"

"I was told it was."

"The person who told you, did they know?"

He looks at me like a lightbulb went off in his brain, grabs my face, and kisses me on the lips. "Thank you."

"What?"

Creed pulls me in and kisses me again. This time I'm prepared and lean in. He hooks his hand around my neck, and his tongue teases mine. The next thing I know, he's standing, laughing, pulling on a t-shirt and boots and walking out of the room, leaving me frustrated, stunned, and wishing he was still kissing me.

Chapter 12

CREED

It's not until I'm on the bottom stair that I realize I kissed Devil, and she kissed me back.

"What's got you smiling?" Reaper smirks and cocks his head to the side.

Holding up a finger, I bound back up the stairs two at a time and open the door to my room.

"Why didn't you lock the door?"

Not giving Devil a chance to answer, I stalk toward her, cup her face, and kiss her again. She moans and returns the kiss.

Pulling away, I smile down at her. "You kissed me."

Her eyes fly open, and she shakes her head. "No, *you* kissed *me*. Three times."

"You counted? And if I'm not mistaken, you kissed me back."

Turning, I walk back to the door.

"Wait! You're leaving?"

I stop in my tracks, a huge grin on my face. "I can't turn around right now, Devil, 'cause if I do, I won't be doing what I need to do. Later, when this mess is under control, I'm going to take you shopping, and we're going to talk about what just happened. Okay?"

"Okay. See you later."

I can hear the smile in her voice, so even though it might break me if I see her beautiful face again, I risk a peek. Devil has her legs drawn up against her body with my t-shirt pulled over them. Her head is tilted to the side, and she has a sexy-as-fuck smile on her face.

"You're killing me."

"See you later." Devil shoos me out of the room.

With a wink, I head back downstairs. Reaper is still there, looking at me as though I've gained a second head.

"I have an idea."

"That's what's got you smiling?"

Looking back up the stairs, I shrug. "Something like that. I'm going to call a meeting with Camilla."

"What?"

"Something doesn't feel right. What's the one thing Camilla cares about?"

"Money," Reaper replies flatly.

"Yeah, I don't think she knows."

"Creed, she sent us."

"Yeah, to escort a shipment, not people." He opens his mouth to interrupt me, but I hold up a hand to silence him. "I'm going to go see her." He tries to argue, but I keep talking. "You're coming with me. Let's go see if the bitch meant to set us up."

***

Camilla is sitting behind her desk. Three of her men stand at the back of the room. She's leaning back, staring at me as if I'm a bug she'd like to squash.

"Do you trust the men in this room?"

"Of course."

"Are they loyal to you?"

Camilla looks past us. "Roberto, leave us and ask Hector to join us."

When he leaves, she says, "Speak."

"The run didn't go as expected."

"Did you get my product?"

"What exactly are we talking about?"

Standing, she leans across the desk. "I swear to God, Creed, if this shipment was short, I will kill you myself."

"Heroin?"

"No, fucking all-day suckers. Yes! Heroin!"

Reaper stands, and the door opens and closes.

"Sit down," hisses Camilla.

I steeple my hands together, and Reaper stares

at Camilla like he could crawl across the desk and gut her. She doesn't flinch. Not many people can withstand a staring contest with Reaper. Camilla obviously doesn't scare easily.

"Reaper, sit." I cross my legs.

Without looking at me, he follows my command, still glaring at her. Camilla takes a seat and settles her eyes on me.

"It wasn't drugs."

She crosses her arms. "What?"

"It was a container full of people."

Her eyebrows come together and her head jerks back. "No, it was heroin."

Shaking my head, I stare at her. Her gaze goes above my head, and she motions for one of her men to come forward. Hector stands next to his boss.

Camilla looks up at him. "Who told you it was an irregular shipment?"

Hector shrugs. "Gabriel."

Camilla pushes her chair back so fast it tips over. She turns, giving us her back, and we all watch as her shoulders rise and fall. Her hands move to her hips.

She turns. "Illegals?" Camilla straightens her jacket and lets her hands fall to her sides.

"Yes."

"Not a drug shipment?"

"No."

She presses her lips together and gives Hector a

scathing look. "Thank you, Creed, for bringing this to me."

"Camilla, so we are clear, we don't–"

"Go. This is an internal matter. It won't happen again."

"No, it won't."

She nods. "I will call you later. Pick up the phone."

Hector gives me a chin lift as I rise from my chair, and Reaper and I walk out of the building.

When we are out of earshot of Camilla and her men, Reaper taps me on the arm. "How'd you know she didn't know?"

Not wanting to tell him it was Devil who led me to figure out Camilla might be in the dark, I shrug. "Gut instinct, but I had to be sure. I needed to see her face when we confronted her."

"Yeah, she sure as shit didn't know. What do you think will happen?"

"The Sanchez family value money above all. Camilla makes the family a lot of money, but Gabriel doesn't. He's selling his own people into God knows what to make a dime. The family kidnap high profile people in Mexico, but they don't sell their own kind. And worst of all, Gabriel must have told someone it was a shipment of heroin to get us to escort it. Which means he knew there was an issue at that warehouse but didn't share the information with anyone. If we'd been killed, Camilla knows the

MC would have rained down on them."
"Meaning it would interrupt their chain of cash?"
"Yep."

Chapter 13

DEVIL

Today has not turned out the way I thought it would. Here I am, sitting in a pool ... Well, sort of. Okay, so not a pool but a body of water. Highway and Feral put a liner in the back of a truck, which to me is a ute, and filled it with water. I'm drinking a margarita Highway made for me, and he even put one of those little umbrellas in it. A group of the MC members are cooking a barbeque, and it smells delicious. Lucy, my new best friend, is next to me drinking a beer. I don't do beer. The music is loud, and I'm having a great day.

Turns out an MC is nothing like I thought it would be. There's a genuine sense of family and loyalty, but there's something else. Something ... wild about them. They remind me of the untamed horses that used to be on my mother's property.

Sometimes they'd get close enough for us to feed them by hand, but we always knew they wouldn't want to be ridden or enclosed.

"Girl, your boobs are bigger than mine. I think you're about to expose yourself to Feral, and he's kind of drooling."

Looking down, I readjust the bikini top Lucy loaned me and look up to see Feral licking his lips.

Ugh.

He's the one member I don't think of as a wild horse. Rabid comes to mind. Yep, he's got Cujo written all over him.

Lucy giggles. "Stop it."

"Stop what?"

"You're glaring at him. Trust me when I tell you, any attention you give him is interpreted as good attention. He's not right."

The sound of Harleys distracts me. Looking over my shoulder, I see Creed and Reaper pulling in.

Lucy nudges me. "You like him?"

"What? No!"

"It's okay to like him. You're on vacation. You're not Vivian, you're Devil. Devil can do anything."

"Can you not tell anyone my real name?"

"Oh honey, I'm never telling anyone. Creed wanted you known as Devil. I'm a little pissed you told me your name. I'm not meant to know."

"Not meant to know what?" Creed stands next to me, staring into what feels like my soul.

"Uhh ... I'm not meant to know–"

"She's not meant to know that I can't drink tequila." The lie flies off my lips so easily and quickly. It must be the alcohol.

Creed swipes my drink and takes a sip. "If I'm not mistaken, margaritas are made with tequila. Why can't you drink it?"

I giggle. "Tequila makes me do crazy things. I'm not me when I drink Tequila."

Creed hands the drink back to me. "I think I might like to see that." He hits the side of the truck. "And you got your pool."

"Highway did it for me."

"I helped." Feral sidles up to the side of the truck.

"Did you?" Creed stares at Feral who is openly ogling my chest.

"Yep, I put the liner in."

Creed waves a hand in front of Feral's face. "Eyes, Feral, avert your eyes."

He immediately steps back and drops his gaze to the ground.

Creed shakes his head and looks at me. "You're distracting."

"I'm sorry. I don't mean to be."

Finishing my drink, I go to get out of the truck.

"What are you doing?"

"I thought you wanted me to cover up?"

Creed smirks. "Nope." He takes my empty glass. "Stay there while I get you another margarita with lots of tequila."

Lucy bursts out laughing, but the laughter dies as Reaper walks past us. He gives her a two-fingered wave and keeps going.

"What is it with you two?"

Lucy swallows what's left of her beer. "Nothing worth talking about."

Her hand goes to her neck, and she watches him walk toward the clubhouse. Before Reaper goes through the doors, he stops and looks back at her. Lucy quickly looks away, but Reaper stands and stares at her.

Without moving my lips, I say, "He's still looking."

"What?"

"He's still looking at you."

Lucy's head snaps up, and Reaper points at her, turns, and walks inside.

"What did *that* mean?"

Lucy shakes her head and climbs out of the truck. "Nothing I want to find out."

Wolf whistles pierce the air as she hurries toward her parked car, dripping wet in her bikini. Creed taps me on the shoulder.

"Where's she going?"

"No idea." He holds out a drink to me and I take it. "What's the deal between those two?"

"Reaper and Lucy?"

I nod.

"Nothing. There's nothing there. Lucy is off limits."

Tilting my head, I take a sip. "You wanna get in?"

Creed grins and closes his eyes, holding his face to the sun. "You like the redneck pool?"

"Oh, yeah."

Creed casts a glance at the people around him. "How'd you get Highway and Feral to do this?"

"I cried."

His head whips so fast in my direction, I nearly drop my glass. "Did someone do something?"

"No. Nothing like that," I reply hastily. "I was sad there wasn't a pool, and I was stuck here and …"

"And you cried."

"Yeah. Justice didn't know what to do, so he got Highway." Stretching out, I grin. "Highway and Feral joined forces and made me happy."

He frowns and points to the men surrounding the firepit and the meat they're cooking. "And that?"

"Oh, Lucy did that. She said it's not a pool party without food."

Creed chuckles. I like the sound. It's making my belly do little flips … or is that the tequila?

"Did you get your business sorted?"

He pins me with a look, and I swear if I wasn't already wet in a pool, I'd have a puddle around me.

"You helped. It got resolved without bloodshed."

He looks at my chest, then his eyes come back to

mine. "Well, at least I think it did. Time will tell." Creed taps the side of the truck. "I'll be back. Don't go anywhere."

He walks away from me, and I notice most of the women are watching him. Creed chats to a few of the men, and there are lots of chin lifts, handshakes, and the occasional punch in the arm. When he's done the rounds, he walks back to me.

"You're turning pink."

"Oh no! I don't tan, I go red, then blister, then peel," I complain as I stand. Moving the bikini top a little to the left, I see a white line. Either side of it is pink. "Dammit!"

Reaching out, I put a hand on Creed's shoulder and try to step out of the truck. In typical me fashion, I slip and fall into his arms.

"I'm so sorry!"

"I'm all wet now, Devil."

He's grinning at me and doesn't seem to mind one little bit that he's getting wet as he carries me across the compound and into the clubhouse. With one arm around his shoulders, I rest my hand on the back of his neck. My fingers stroke the skin there, and those flips in my belly turn into full-blown somersaults. Creed keeps walking up the stairs and into his room, where he puts me on the floor. His warm hands rest on my waist as we stand in his room.

He leans in, and my breath catches as he sweeps

stray hairs off my face.

Creed lowers his head to mine and whispers, "Go shower."

Feeling as though he's playing with me, I take a step back out of his reach, put a hand on my hip, and wave a hand up and down. "I still don't have any clothes."

"Right."

"You promised to take me shopping."

"So I did." Creed takes a step back. "Go shower. I'll find something for you to wear and we'll go shopping."

I raise my arms in victory. "Yes!"

Creed's eyes go to my boobs, and I instantly drop my arms. With his head tilted to the side, he closes the gap between us, his rough hands gripping my upper arms, and kisses me. Not like this morning. This kiss is demanding, forceful, and he walks me backward until I hit a wall. One leg goes between my thighs, and I part my legs for him as his hands roam my body. Electricity courses through my veins, sending pulses of pleasure wherever his hands explore.

A groan escapes me when his fingers tweak my nipple, and I arch into him, needing so much more. Creed drags his mouth down my neck, his teeth and stubble eliciting fireworks like I've never felt before as he works his way further down.

His mouth covers my nipple, and his tongue

swirls over it, causing it to pebble. When he sucks on my flesh, I think I'm ready to come then and there. My body responds to each flick of his tongue, and when he slides his hands between my legs, I spread them further apart, wanting so much more. Need and want are all I can think about.

Creed tugs on the bikini bottoms and rips them from me. I gasp, and he kisses me, his tongue dancing with mine. My hands go under his t-shirt, exploring hard, toned skin. Creed growls when I dig my nails in, and the sound reverberates through my whole body.

"Open your eyes, Devil." Instantly, I do as I'm told. "Good girl."

His thumb presses on my nub, and I moan at the unexpected pleasure.

"Do you like that?"

"Oh, yes." Closing my eyes, I twist my head to the side, concentrating on the building pressure between my legs, I grind against his hand.

"Open your eyes." Instantly, I open them. "Close them again and you won't finish."

His eyes bore into mine and I'm transfixed by their depths. They've gone dark, and lust filled as he kisses his way down my body. His mouth suckles on my nub, and I cry out in pleasure.

"Yes!"

Creed chuckles, picks me up, and puts me in the middle of his bed. With wild abandon, I spread my legs wide, hoping he'll use his mouth on me again. He takes off his cut and puts it on a chair.

"Keep those pretty green eyes on me, Devil."

"I will."

Creed crawls over me, his face an inch from mine. He kisses me with his eyes open and slowly weaves a trail of desire from my mouth to my pussy as he licks, sucks, and teases me. All the while his eyes keep checking to see if mine are open.

Honestly, there's no way I couldn't watch him. He's sexy, demanding, and my body is responding to every little thing he does. Like a man possessed, his mouth covers my pussy. Creed's tongue dives between my folds, but when he sucks on my nub and his chin moves, I swear I'm about to shatter from the sensation.

Spreading my legs further apart, I grip the sheet above my head and move my hips in rhythm with his tongue. My thighs feel like they are on fire as I search for my release. Creed inserts a finger, and I lose his mouth as he watches himself moving in and out of me.

"More," I beg.

"You want to finish?"

"Please."

His finger curls up inside of me as he moves it in and out, and my body shudders.

"Please," I plead again.

Creed looks at me, his eyes nearly black and then

slowly kisses all around my pussy, but not in the spot I need him to be.

"Creed!" I growl.

His tongue flicks over my nub, and then his mouth descends upon me. Creed sucks as his tongue works me into a frenzy. I thread my hands through his hair to hold him in place as I grind into his face and reach for my release.

With my head arched back, my body rocking against Creed's face, the whole world crashes around me as wave after wave of pleasure runs through me. My hands go limp and fall to my sides, with hooded lids, I watch as he wipes his face on the sheet then kisses his way to my lips.

"You did good, Devil."

"Tequila."

Creed holds himself above me, a frown on his face. "What?"

"I told you, I do crazy things on tequila."

"Right. So, this was because of the tequila?"

"Uh-huh."

He nods, climbs off the bed and folds his arms across his chest. "Go shower and I'll take you into town."

Confused, I sit up. "But you didn't–"

"No, I didn't. See you downstairs."

Chapter 14

CREED

The look on her face as I leave my room makes me feel like an ass. But being told she only did what she did because of tequila doesn't do anything for my manhood. My dick is hard enough to hammer nails.

I head straight for the kitchen and run my head under some cold water to ease my hard-on.

Missy steps up next to me and holds out a dish towel. "You okay, Creed?"

"I'm good." Standing, I readjust myself, take the towel, and wipe my face.

Missy looks at my crotch and licks her lips. "Is there anything you need help with?"

Fucking Missy would be a mistake, but my dick doesn't seem to care right now. Stepping closer, she reaches out and grabs my cock. As soon as she rubs up and down, I know I've made a huge mistake.

Pulling her hand away, I hold it up and shake my head.

"No one will know," she whispers.

"I will know." Shoving her away from me, I throw the dish towel on the bench and stalk out of the kitchen and back to my room.

The shower is going, and my dick becomes harder at the thought of Devil wet, soapy, and naked in the shower. The water stops running, and Devil comes out wrapped in a towel, her blond hair in a messy bun on her head.

She walks past me and sits on the bed. "Why'd you leave?"

Without turning around to face her, I say, "Tequila."

"I don't understand."

"I guess you got your holiday fling."

"Creed, I've had sex with exactly one person, and he left me for my best friend. I thought it was good sex, or at least I thought it would get better with time. But he never made me melt like you just did. The tequila didn't make me have sex with you, but it helped give me the courage to let you carry me up here and ..." Her voice trails off.

When I turn around, she's looking at her hands. "And what?"

"I thought we were having a good time, and you left."

"Do you know who I am?"

"You're Creed, President of the Royal Bastards MC, Jacksonville. Highway says you're a good guy."

"Highway says? What do *you* think?"

"I think you could have killed me, and you didn't." Devil glances up at me then back at her hands. "But the way you're looking at me right now, I think you're regretting that decision."

This woman will be the end of me. Bending, I kneel in front of her and place my hands on her knees. "Vivian Lewis, I like you. I want you to like me. I don't want tequila to be the reason you do."

She cups her hand around my face. "I like it when you say my name. I like it better when you call me Devil."

Devil moves her thumb across my cheek to my lips and kisses me. Moving forward, I push her back on the bed and kiss her. Devil laughs and turns her head to the side, breaking our connection.

"Wait."

"No," I growl, kissing her collarbone.

"Creed." Her voice has gone serious, so I stop and look down at her.

"Devil?"

"You said you like me?"

"Hmm?"

"Creed, you said you *like* me."

"Yes."

"Can you get off of me for a sec?"

I roll over, and Devil scrambles away from me.

The towel falls off, but she sits with her back against the headboard and covers herself with the towel.

"I'm here for six weeks. I know this is probably something you do all the time but–"

"It isn't."

"Let me speak."

Nodding, I reposition myself to face her. "Okay."

"I'm here for six weeks, and we seem to get along. Creed, I know you don't know me, but I'm a good person. I'm loyal. I thought ... for the next six weeks you could show me around and," she pauses and looks down at the towel, "and maybe for six weeks I could be yours. Only yours. And ... and you could be m-mine."

Moving closer to her, I put my hand on her knee. "I don't share."

Her eyes meet mine. "You don't?"

"No. Sure, some of the women here will fuck anyone, but I've never claimed someone. I'm claiming you."

"You are?"

"Yeah." My lips press against hers, and Devil releases the towel to deepen the kiss.

She pushes me onto my back and straddles me. My dick strains against my jeans, and when she rocks her hips against mine, I feel it in my balls. In one swift movement, I roll us over and move off of her to stand next to the bed.

"Creed?"

"Give me a second."

First, I kick off my boots, then my jeans, and lastly, I pull my t-shirt over my head. Opening the drawer of my bedside table, I pull out a condom, rip it open with my teeth, and roll it on. Devil crawls across the bed and puts her hand around my cock, pumping it up and down.

"Need your pussy or your mouth."

Devil grins up at me and moves up the mattress, spreading her legs wide. She's beautiful, uninhibited, and after this, she'll be mine. Grabbing one leg, I pull her back toward me.

"Creed!"

"All good things come to those who wait."

"Well, fuck me then."

I grin and kiss the inside of her thigh. She smells like apples. Trailing kisses along her creamy skin, I flick my tongue over her clit, and she gasps.

"Are your eyes open?"

"Wide open," she purrs.

My cock is thick, and I don't want to hurt her, so I need to know she's ready for me. Devil entwines her fingers in my hair and grinds into my face as I suck on her clit. Her movements become more erratic when I slip two fingers into her slick heat.

"I'm coming," Devil whispers, almost too softly for me to hear.

She moans, and her arms go limp at her sides as the orgasm washes through her. This time, I'm going to claim her. Lifting one leg, I kiss her calf and place it on my shoulder.

"Put your other leg up."

Devil does, her eyes never leaving mine. Using my hand, I guide my cock into her. She gasps at the new invasion. Slowly, I pull out and sink back inside her.

"I won't break."

"Don't want to hurt you."

"You won't." To prove her point, Devil rolls her hips.

I push her legs down and lie on top of her. I attempt to be gentle, but when she reaches up and bites my chest, I'm done for. Planting my hands on either side of her head, I pound into her. Devil wraps her legs around me, meeting me thrust for thrust as she rakes her nails down my back.

"Not enough," she demands with a frustrated gasp.

Devil plants a foot on the bed and rolls us to climb on top of me. With a sigh of pleasure, she impales herself on my dick, taking all of me into her. Devil threads her fingers with mine as she rides me. A look of concentration crosses her beautiful face as she searches once again for her orgasm.

"Devil, let me help."

Not breaking her rhythm, she looks at me.

"Let my hands go, baby."

Immediately, she moves her hands to my chest,

her nails digging into my flesh, sending pleasure straight to my cock. There's nothing like a little pain with pleasure. I put one of my hands on her hip and move her faster while the other goes to her swollen clit. A furrow creases her brow, her mouth drops open, and she cries out as her pussy milks my cock.

When it subsides, she goes limp and collapses on top of me, so I roll us, pull out, put her on her stomach, and then drag her toward the edge of the bed. Devil is like a rag-doll, but she pushes up onto her knees. When she's in position, I plunge back into her slick, tight pussy. She cries out and pushes herself against me. Gripping her ass, I pound into her again and again. My balls begin to tingle, and I know I'm close.

Devil's body shudders as another orgasm rips through her. Finally, my own release overwhelms me. Electricity courses through my veins as she impales herself on my cock again and again. A roar escapes me as wave after wave of pleasure rocks my system. I dig my fingers into her flesh, and I'm certain she'll have a few bruises after this. It pleases me, knowing she'll have my marks on her beautiful body. Sliding a hand up to the base of her neck, I grip her hair and pull her up to bring her back flush with my chest.

"Mine."

***

We made love four times. I've never had a woman respond to my touch or demands so completely. I can't get enough of her, and Devil seems to feel the same way. It's night, the air is cooler, and she's snoozing with her head on my stomach. Reaching down, I sweep her hair off her face.

"No more. I need food."

"And clothes."

Her eyes open. "You taking me out, Creed?"

"Yeah."

Devil sits upright and stretches. I trace a path down her side and marvel at how beautiful she is, naked and mine.

"I need to shower, Creed. I need shoes and something to wear too."

Tracing lines along her side, I nod. "Yeah. You can wear one of my t-shirts. Let me see what I can find."

Devil giggles and swats at my hands. "First, we need to shower."

"I like the sound of that."

"No, no, no. I'm showering alone while you find me something to wear."

"It'll be more fun if I help you shower."

With her pretty, green eyes focused on my chest, she chews her lip for a moment and finally meets my gaze. "I need food and clothing and only you can provide that for me, so go get it."

Moving quickly, I pin her to the bed and nip her

lip. "Woman, you're lucky I like you." I climb out of bed and pull on some jeans.

Devil sits up. "Nothing sexier than a man in jeans and bare feet."

"I'll remember that."

She winks and does a slow, sultry walk into the bathroom.

"Devil, you keep walking like that and we're never leaving this room."

She giggles and shuts the door.

Yep, she's going to be the end of me.

CREED

Devil wanted to go to a department store first. I'm waiting for her outside a changing room in Dillard's, trying to look comfortable. She grabbed a whole heap of lingerie, and I'm wishing I was in there with her. Devil is beautiful naked, but thoughts of her dressed up in something provocative and only for me, makes my cock harden.

After what feels like forever, Devil walks out with an arm full of underwear, most of them black or white. As her sales are rung up, I hand over my credit card.

"No!"

"Yes," I reply forcefully.

"Creed, it's too much!"

Shaking my head at her, I wrap an arm around

her waist and pull her to me as the cashier finishes the sale and hands the bagged items to me. On tiptoe, Devil tilts her head back and kisses me.

"Am I going to like what you've bought?"

She flutters her lashes. "Maybe. There might be one or two sexy pieces in there, along with comfy undies."

"Right."

"Creed, is that you?"

Turning around, I stop in my tracks as my blood runs cold. Hector is walking toward us with a couple of his men

Quietly, so only Devil can hear, I say, "Keep your mouth shut."

"Hector." I force myself to smile and dip my chin toward him.

"I didn't think your kind went shopping."

"My kind? How do you think we get groceries, Hector?"

He raises his eyebrows in surprise, then laughs and lightly slaps my arm. "Come, come, I was only teasing." He looks Devil up and down. "Aren't you going to introduce me?"

Hector holds out his hand to Devil, but I step in front of her. He steps back in surprise, and I realize I've made a mistake. Showing I care about someone is a weakness, one the cartel can exploit.

Hector looks around me and grins at Devil. "Hello."

"G'day."

Hector pins me with a look. I turn, grab Devil by the arm, and walk her in the opposite direction.

"I told you not to speak."

"I'm sorry! I was being polite."

We walk out of the store and keep moving until we hit Target. Devil pulls out of my grasp.

"I said I was sorry."

Dropping the bag, I cup her face in my hands and kiss her. "I'm sorry." I lean back and look into her eyes. "Hector works for the person who wanted you dead." The color drains out of her face. "It's okay."

"I said g'day. I couldn't get more Aussie if I tried. Do they know I'm Australian?"

"Yes. Their mule would have told them everything about you."

"You mean Ria?"

"Yeah."

"Take me back to the compound."

Turning her around, I grab her hand and pull her into Target. "You need clothes. Don't get me wrong, Devil, I like seeing you in my t-shirts, but I'm sure you'll be sick of them after a few days."

"What about Hector?"

"I doubt Hector or any of his men have ever stepped inside a Target store."

"So we're safe?"

"Except you've only got one hour before they close."

Devil turns and power walks into the women's section.

"I need a trolley!" she shouts over her shoulder.

"A what?"

"A trolley."

"What the hell is a trolley?"

"You know, something to put my stuff in to wheel it to the checkout?"

"You mean a shopping cart?"

"You Americans are weird." Devil begins going through the dresses in front of her.

When she finds her size, she hangs it over her arm. Turning, I walk to the front of the store. Standing just inside is Hector.

"You didn't kill her?"

"She was innocent. It was a mistake."

"You were told to get rid of her."

I cross my arms over my chest. "She's not a threat."

Hector steps closer to me. "She knows too much."

"She's with me."

Hector steps back and laughs. "Oh, that's perfect. Camilla is going to slice off your balls for fun."

"Camilla doesn't need to know."

Hector puffs out his cheeks and looks at me as though I'm deranged.

"She's only here for a few weeks, and then she's on a plane back home. She's not a threat."

"What's going to stop her from calling the cops once she gets there? Nothing, that's what. Jesus, Creed, I thought you were smarter than that."

"Hector, I'm telling you, she's not a threat."

Hector nods, purses his lips, and turns to leave, only to spin on his heel and face me again. "She's staying at your compound?"

"Yes."

"You'll vouch for her?"

"Yes."

He looks through the doors into Target. "Okay. It's simple. You can have her until it's time for her to leave, and then you end her. No loose ends. The Diablos don't do loose ends." He raises a brow. "Are we good?"

I nod. "We're good."

Hector gives me a chin lift and disappears into the night. I grab a shopping cart and walk back to Devil.

Chapter 16

DEVIL

The Escalade is full of bags of clothing, shoes, and toiletries. Creed paid for all of it, although I protested. He said I could pay from here on out, but he was going to take care of me.

It felt amazing to hear him say that to me. Todd certainly never paid for anything. He was more of a taker than a giver.

I've been so lost in my thoughts that I hadn't even realized we've ridden in silence until I look up and Creed's pulling into the clubhouse parking lot.

"You okay?"

"Sorry, I'm miles away."

He opens the door but remains seated as a crease forms between his brows. "Thinking about home?"

"A little."

We both climb out of the Escalade and meet at the back, where he opens the back hatch. I reach inside, pick up several bags, and begin walking toward the building. While Creed locks the car, I wait for him at the clubhouse stairs.

"Hungry?"

As if on cue, my stomach growls. "Yeah."

"I'll order Chinese. Is there anything you'd like?"

"Fried rice."

We walk through the clubhouse, and a feeling of belonging washes over me as though this is normal. Creed opens the door to his room and moves past me to put my bags on the bed.

"I'll go order something. Will you be okay here by yourself?"

Looking at the bags on the bed, I nod. "It's going to take me a minute to unpack all of this."

Creed takes the bags off me and puts them on the bed with the others. He cups my face in his hands and kisses me. A tingle of excitement floods through my system, but he pulls away.

"I'll be back. I'm going to go order food. You relax and put this away."

"Are you saying I can have room in your closet?"

Creed chuckles. "Yeah, and the drawers and anywhere else you'd like."

"Next, you'll be giving me keys to your room, and then you're in trouble," I tease, as I grin at him.

"Oh, Devil, I'm already in trouble." He winks at

me, kisses my nose, and walks out of the room.

Staring at all the bags on the bed, I go in search of the sleep shorts and top with the pale-pink flowers all over them. Of course, I find them in the last bag I search through. Stripping out of my clothes, I put them on and begin putting away my stuff. When I'm finished, I open Creed's door and poke my head out to find an empty hallway. Lucy opens the door across the hall and comes out holding her shoes. Her eyes lock with mine, and she quickly shuts the door.

"Hey, whatcha doin'?" Lucy tries to rake her fingers through her tangled hair.

"I need food."

Lucy drops her shoes on the floor and puts them on. "Come on, I'll take you to the kitchen."

Shaking my head, I say, "Creed left to go order Chinese, but he hasn't come back."

"Okay, what if we go to the kitchen and find something to tide you over?"

"Ice cream?"

Lucy laughs and crooks a finger at me. "Come on."

Following closely behind her, I brace myself for what's to come as we go downstairs and walk past the bar. Just as I thought, the MC members who are present wolf whistle and openly stare at us. Unlike Lucy, I find it hard to ignore them, so I keep my eyes glued to her back. When we are alone in the kitchen,

I breathe a sigh of relief.

"You get used to it." She opens the freezer. "You want chocolate or vanilla?"

"Those are my choices?"

"Yep."

"Chocolate."

Lucy winks at me, pulls it from the freezer, and nods to the other side of the room. "Bowls are in that cupboard. I'll get the spoons."

Sitting on a stool near the kitchen bench, Lucy digs a spoon into the chocolatey goodness. I push both bowls closer to her, and she scoops out the ice cream.

"Whose room were you in?"

Lucy shrugs. "No one special."

The door to the kitchen opens, and Missy walks into the room. "Oh great, if it isn't the stuck-up bitches."

"Shut your pie hole, Missy." Lucy points a spoon at her.

"You going to make me?"

Lucy bursts out laughing. "Honey, you are drunk and just plain nasty. I wouldn't waste my time on you."

Missy stares at us, then her face twists into a scowl. "You think you're so good, catching the eye of Reaper? Thinking you're hot stuff nabbing the VP will do that to ya. We've all been there. You're nothing special, Lucy, and you're no fucking diamond."

Lucy shoves a spoonful of ice cream into her mouth and shakes her head. "Aww, poor Missy. Always available for a fuck, but never gonna be anyone's ol' lady, and we all know it."

"At least I know what I am, and I'm not pretending to be anything else."

Lucy rolls her eyes. "I know who I am. I know what I want. Unlike you, I'm not waiting around for a man to pick me. Unlike you, I'm not pathetic."

Missy screams and runs toward Lucy, her arms raised as though she's going to strangle her. Lucy and I move, and stools topple over as Missy launches herself at us. The kitchen door bursts open and Creed storms in.

"What the fuck?"

Missy isn't deterred and continues screaming like a banshee as she tries to climb over the stools while Lucy laughs and I hide behind Creed.

"Missy!" Creed yells. "What the fuck are you doing?"

She stops moving. "She thinks she's better than me. She said she's better than me!"

"Fuck me." Creed's eyes go to Lucy. "Well?"

"I did not say I was better than her."

Creed quirks a brow in my direction.

I shake my head. "No, she didn't."

Missy bursts into tears. "She called me pathetic."

Creed looks at Lucy, me, and finally back at

Missy. "Go home, Missy."

"B-But–"

"Go home," he repeats more forcefully.

She nods as fresh tears stream down her cheeks. As she stumbles from the room, she purposely hits Lucy with her shoulder.

Creed throws his hands in the air. "You know how she is. Did you have to torment her?"

"The woman is wacked, Creed. You know it, and I know it. We were in here eating ice cream when she started her shit." Lucy cocks out a hip and waves a hand dismissively.

"I don't care."

Reaper walks through the door. "Is everything okay?"

"Missy," Lucy replies with a sneer.

"The bitch is wacked." Reaper grins, and I find it amusing they both called her the same thing.

Creed holds up a hand. "From where I stand, she isn't the only one. Lucy, watch yourself."

He grabs my hand and pulls me through the door and up the stairs to his room. Once the door is closed, I climb into bed.

"Ice cream?"

"I wanted something sweet."

Creed laughs and looks at the ceiling and back at me. "You're sweet. You taste like apples and smell like–"

"It's the shower gel."

"The shower gel has nothing to do with it." He scrubs a hand over his face. "You smell like home to me. It's been a long time since I've felt this way."

With his hands in his pockets, Creed looks tormented as he stares at me from across the room.

I beckon him toward me. "Come here."

Frowning at me, he takes a step and stops. "What am I going to do?"

"I could leave?"

"No, you can't." Creed reaches into his pocket and pulls out my phone. "You should call your mom. Let her know you're okay."

"I am okay, aren't I, Creed?"

He moves next to the bed and holds out my phone. "So long as you are under my roof, no one will hurt you."

Smiling up at him, I take my phone, but he doesn't smile back. Creed stands there like an immoveable statue or a ruler trying to decide the best course of action. Kneeling on the bed, I wrap my arms around him and, like a man possessed, he responds by holding me tightly.

He traces circles on my back with one hand, and I stroke his hair. We are locked together, each trying to give the other comfort. A knock at the door breaks us apart, and he moves to see who it is. I'm left feeling alone as I sit on the bed, wishing he was still holding me.

Creed opens the door to Reaper on the other side.

"Winchester is here, Prez. There's an issue with one of the strip clubs."

Creed looks over his shoulder at me and nods. "I'm on my way." Closing the door, he leans against it. "You okay up here?"

"I'd be better if you were with me and if I had food."

"Ahh, shit. I forgot." He shrugs. "Work," he says by way of explanation and pushes off the door. "I'll send out a prospect to get you something. Sorry, it won't happen again."

"Is everything okay?"

Creed stares into my eyes and lifts his chin.

"You feel it too, don't you, Creed?"

"From the moment I laid eyes on you."

My heart beats a little faster. "Go work. I'll be here when you get back."

He smiles at me, the torment from a moment ago seemingly disappearing. "Your food will be here within the hour."

"Okay."

He sighs. "Are you going to be okay?"

"I'll be fine. If I need anything, I'll find Highway."

He nods. "Okay, I'll tell him to hang close to the clubhouse."

Creed makes no move to leave, so I walk across the room and wrap my arms around him. "Work. Go work." I kiss his lips.

He kisses me back, holding on to me almost painfully. "You smell like home."

Creed kisses me again and disappears downstairs.

Chapter 17

CAMILLA

I've left Hector in charge while I'm gone. He's a good soldier and knows how I like things run. He doesn't always agree with me, but he will never publicly go against me. When the doors are closed and it's only us, we argue. Having witnessed the struggles I've faced as a woman in this business, Hector understands how important it is for me to save face in front of the men.

His family has worked for my family for a long time. It's how it is in our industry. One day, if Hector ever has children, they will work for us too. His father was my father's closest confidant. When he was killed, we all felt the loss.

The family jet touches down in Mexico City. The bump as the tires hit the asphalt causes me to spill my drink. As soon as we are cleared, I'll walk to the hangar where our helicopter is, and someone will fly me to my father. He has a small estate surrounded by a stone wall and more security than the Pope. Of course, he has places in Mexico where he conducts business, but when he needs peace and quiet, he goes to Casa Santuario, which means "sanctuary house."

Finally, the pilot opens the door to the jet. Picking up my briefcase, I walk down the stairs where I'm met by some of my father's men. My whole life I've been escorted wherever I've needed to go. Security and muscle have always been my way of life. When I was thirteen, a rival drug lord kidnapped me. My father moved heaven and earth to get me back. Since that day, I swore I'd never be someone's puppet again. For my fourteenth birthday, I asked for a gun and for someone to teach me how to shoot. For my fifteenth birthday, self-defense classes. I'll never be helpless again.

"Señora Sanchez, it's good to have you home."

"Marco, how many times have I asked you to call me Camilla?"

He smiles and shrugs. "Many, but it doesn't feel right."

"How is he?" My father is a difficult man, and Marco reads his moods better than most.

"Arguing with your mother over what color to paint the bedroom."

"Mom's redecorating again?"

Marco nods and raises his eyebrows. It's a sign she's discovered he has yet another mistress. Every time my mother redecorates, it's a way for her to put her stamp on our family home, making it perfectly clear she is the only Señorita Sanchez, and will not be replaced.

Mom shouldn't worry. Dad's flings are something he does to prove he's a man. He never keeps them long and will never divorce my mother. He loves her. I've never doubted his affections for the mother of his children but, like most men, he likes the thrill of the chase.

Marco guides me through the airport toward a hangar where we keep the helicopter. We aren't bothered by any of the employees as we walk. They are paid well and don't give us much attention. When we are close to the hangar, Marco moves ahead of me to open the door to the helicopter.

Once I'm inside, they start the pre-flight checklist, and I buckle myself in.

"Who's at the house?"

"Seems everyone has come home. All your father's captains are there."

"And Gabriel?"

Marco lifts his chin. "He should arrive tomorrow."

"Good."

Marco gives me the side-eye, but he's been around my family long enough not to ask too many questions. He knows Gabriel and I have always had our differences.

The flight takes a little over half an hour. When we touch down on the circular driveway in front of the house, Marco opens the door and waits for me. I've been in and out of helicopters since I was a kid, but every time I walk under the rotor blades, I duck and run.

My mother waves at me from the double front doors of our home. I rush up the stairs and into her arms.

"Mija, so good to have you home."

"Mamá, you look beautiful." Holding her elbow, I take a moment to appreciate the woman standing before me.

My mother is in her sixties, although I do not know her exact age because she has never revealed it to me. Her long, dark hair is swept up in a chignon and, like me, she's wearing a black pantsuit. I chose a red silk blouse, but she's wearing a cream top. I like to think I get my sense of style from my mother and my head for business from my father.

"Your father is in the den. He's been waiting for you." She pats my hand, resting hers over the top of mine. "I think he wants to talk to you." She lowers her voice and leans in as though we're conspirators. "Between you and me, he's struck a deal with the Alvarez family. Soon, the conflicts will be over and we'll be in the balance of power, all thanks to you and your union."

"Oh, Mamá." I shake my head in disbelief.

"Don't be like that, Camilla. I've been planning your wedding day for a long time."

"Yes, Mamá." It's easier to agree with her than start an argument.

I learned how to manipulate my mother a long time ago. There will be no wedding between me and the Alvarez family, especially not with the second son of Emilio Alvarez. If I were going to marry anyone, it would be his oldest son, Cruz. Everyone knows he's tipped to take over when Emilio steps down. For me to marry a lesser son is an insult to me.

We stop at the closed doors of the den, and my mother embraces me. "Please don't upset your father. He's been looking forward to having you home." She kisses me on the cheek and holds me at arm's length for a moment before disappearing into the house.

I wait until I can't hear her footsteps on the polished timber floors before I knock on the door.

"Come in."

I open the door and am surprised at how many men are in the room. Marco wasn't exaggerating when he said all of dad's captains were home. Most of them are my father's age but, as with any organization, there are a couple of fresh faces.

"Camilla!" Papá smiles and steps around his desk

to hug me.

"Papá."

He slips his arm around my waist and guides me behind his desk, where two chairs await us. He takes one and I take the other.

"Does your mother know you are here?"

"Yes, Papá. She met me at the chopper."

"Do you know everyone?" He holds out a hand to the rest of the room.

"Yes." I smile at them, and they all sit.

"Good, good. You're home to discuss business?"

"In private, Papá. It can wait."

"If it's something that affects us, we should all know," Santiago replies.

"Yes, if it was something that affected you, I'd tell you," I say sweetly.

He knows I have no intention of telling him anything. Most of these men have known me since I was a child, and a few of them think they can tell me what to do. They can't, and every once in a while, I'm forced to let them know I answer to no one.

Santiago smiles. "Good."

Ignoring him, I look at my father. "Is everything okay?"

"Yes. We've been discussing a merger between us and the Alvarez family. One that will mean no more bloodshed." He twists in his chair and faces me. "It's what's best for the family, for all of us."

Yeah, what's best for all of them, but not what's best for me. Now is not the time for me to speak out. This will take careful planning. So, like the dutiful daughter I am, I plaster a smile on my face. Santiago is the only one in the room not smiling. He's staring at me as though he can tell what I'm thinking. He'll be the one to avoid. Santiago has wanted my Florida run since the moment I secured routes, and it became one of the most profitable. It took a long time to find the most vulnerable people within law enforcement and pay them to help us run drugs over the border or intimidate them. Not every interaction was successful, and every setback took its toll on the bottom line, but it's worked for the past three years.

"Gentlemen, now that my daughter is here, how about we break for an early dinner? Drinks by the pool until we feast."

It's my father's subtle way of telling them he wants alone time with me and they are all excused. Some look relieved, while others appear to be annoyed. Santiago looks amused.

"Of course, Mateo. Enjoy time with your girl, for she won't be yours forever." Santiago winks at me and is the first out of the room.

I watch them all go and when I look at my father, his eyes are on me as though he's trying to read my mood.

"How are you, mija?"

"Papá, I have something I need to talk to you about." Twisting slightly, I face him.

"Your mother told you?" He raises his eyebrows and smacks his lips together.

"What? No."

"It's for the best."

Great, he thinks I'm upset about my union with the Alvarez family. I am, but that's not what I need to talk to him about.

"Papá, I need you to *listen* to me."

"I know he's not what you wanted. But in time, he could become that man." He's not talking to me like he would a captain, but as his daughter, and I've had enough.

"Papá, Gabriel is running illegals across the border," I blurt out.

"What? No. He wouldn't. He knows better."

Gently, I place my hand over his. "Gabriel contacted me and said he was moving a shipment of heroin, but things weren't in place over the border. He needed someone to protect the shipment. I asked the Royal Bastards in Jacksonville to take care of it."

"Creed is a good man."

"Yes."

"Go on." He pulls back from me and steeples his fingers together. This is the pose he undertakes when he evaluates someone. I've seen him do it a thousand times to his men, but never once for me.

Sitting straighter in the chair, I look him in the eyes. "When Creed got there, it was a container full of our people. Mostly women, mostly dead."

His lips turn down in a frown. "I'm not happy with his infraction, but he's trying to find his feet. He doesn't have your head for business."

"No, he doesn't, but it wasn't his first time. Gabriel has been doing this for the better part of a year. Running illegals is dangerous. Too many things can go wrong, and his man on the other side was butchered, so he's pissed off a rival. My guess is the Russians."

He stands abruptly, his chair smashing against the wall behind him. "He knows better."

"Clearly, he doesn't."

With both hands planted on his desk, he leans forward. "I cut him off. I told him he needed to be more like you. This is my fault."

"Papá, this is not your fault. Gabriel is weak, he always has been." I stand and walk around the desk to face him. "What do I have to do to prove to you I'm the stronger child?"

His face is tilted down, but he moves his eyes to look at me.

"Papá, I'm not a man, but I rule like one. You taught me that. You gave me the ambition and the foresight to find a trade route from the border to Florida to West Virginia. I have plans, Papá, ones where we increase our fentanyl distribution."

He moves his head and focuses his gaze on me. "And what will we do with the poppy fields if you increase fentanyl distribution?"

"Nothing. We'll make it cheaper. Eventually, they'll come back to it, and then we will have won, Papá."

He nods and examines me up and down. "Make it cheaper?"

"Yes, we won't make as much money in the short term, but in the long term? We'll rake it in."

"You have a chemist for your fentanyl?"

"Yes. Several."

"You did this without talking to me?"

I shake my head vehemently. "I would never do anything like this without your blessing. Yes, things are in place, but if you say no, the whole thing can fade away. If my projections are correct, and I think they are, within three years we'll be doing almost double what we are right now."

"Only three years?"

"Yes."

"Send me your projections. As for your brother, leave him to me."

"Of course, Papa. As always, I'm happy to do as you wish."

My father straightens his stance, crosses his arms over his chest, and nods. Maybe it's wishful thinking on my part, but I think he finally sees me as an equal and not as a woman who's playing in a man's world.

Leaving his office, I head for my room, only to find Santiago waiting for me in the hallway. He's leaning against the wall, checking his fingernails.

"Don't you look smug?" He doesn't look up from inspecting his hand, as though I'm the most unimportant person he's ever met.

"Santiago Estrada, what can I do for you?"

"You've weaseled your way out of the marriage, haven't you?" He pushes off the wall and walks toward me.

"I hope so."

"It's a good union for the family."

"Then *you* marry him."

Santiago laughs. "He'd probably like me better."

"Yes, he probably would."

"One of these days I'm going to get Florida from you." Santiago walks away from me and down the hall.

"Over my cold, dead body."

He pauses, holds up a hand, waggles a finger at me, and keeps going. There's no way I'll ever willingly let Santiago take what's mine. Well, there is *one* way. When I'm head of the Diablo Cartel, I'll give it to him as an act of good faith.

***

My father called a family meeting as soon as Gabriel

arrived. From the way my mother stared at me, he's about to announce my engagement. My heart is beating so fast in my chest, I feel like a rabbit caught in a snare. There's no way I can avoid marrying if my father wants it to happen. Gabriel smiles smugly. I bet he's thrilled at the thought I'm about to be sold like a brood mare.

Papá is already in his seat behind his ornate desk. I used to hide underneath it when I was a child.

There's no hiding today.

Putting on my best fake smile, I move to sit in one of the armchairs facing Papa, but he shakes his head and pats the seat next to him. It's unusual for him to want me there for a family meeting, but I suppose he wants to play the good father by patting my hand or hugging me when he tells me my good news.

"Sofia, my love, would you mind leaving us alone?"

My mother looks at me. "I thought we'd be discussing–"

Papá holds up a hand. "Please, my love, we have business to discuss."

"You said it was a family meeting."

"It is. But first, business."

My mother gives me a forced, tight smile, devoid of warmth, and walks from the room.

"So, Papá, are we all here to announce Camilla's

engagement?" Gabriel beams at me brazenly.

He knows I don't want to get married, and he was furious when I turned a profit on the Florida route. He, like all the men associated with the Diablo Cartel, thinks a woman's place is in the home, barefoot and pregnant.

"Not exactly." My father leans forward, staring at my brother. "Tell me about your transport business."

Gabriel instantly looks at me. "What would you like to know?"

"It has come to my attention you are running our people across the border."

"I pay my dues to the family," Gabriel states defiantly.

"On the backs of your own people?"

"What has she told you, Papá?"

My father sits back, looks at me, and gestures for me to speak.

"You told Hector it was a drug run. I sent the Royal Bastards to escort the shipment, but it turned out to be people. Most of whom were dead."

"It turns a profit."

Standing, I lean over the desk the same way my father does. "These are our people! It's the one thing we *don't* do."

Gabriel jumps to his feet. "Don't you dare talk to me like this!" He throws one hand in the air. "It's no worse than the poison you peddle."

In a steely tone, my father says, "But it is."

We look at him. My father grew up poor. When he was eleven, a group of men came to the small village where he lived and took all the women, including his mother. These women were sold into slavery or prostitution. He never saw his mother again.

Papá can be a hard, vicious man. He believes in loyalty. If someone betrays that loyalty, he'll end them. No second chances. If they fuck him over once, they don't get to do it again.

"Papá?" All the anger leaves Gabriel's voice as he stares at our father.

"Sit down."

Gabriel and I both sit. Papá reaches over and pats my leg.

"Your sister is twice the man you are."

"You gave her the Florida route when it should have been mine!"

A scowl settles on my face. "No one gave me anything. I fought for it, I bled for it, and I'm the one who made it work. But what do you do? You bitch and complain like a spoiled child and take the easy road, even though you know how Papá feels about it. You're nothing but a disappointment."

Gabriel stands. "Are you going to let her talk to me like this, Papá?"

My father quirks an eyebrow. "Yes. Your sister is right. I gave you everything, Gabriel. You were supposed to be the one to take over for me, but you don't have a head for business like Camilla does."

Gabriel's eyes bulge, and his mouth falls open. "She's a *woman*!"

"True, but we've all underestimated her."

"You promised her to the Alvarez family. If you break that deal, we'll have a war on our hands. Give me her arm of the business and I promise to make you proud."

Anger rears up inside me, and I slam my hand on the desk. "See, that's the difference between us, Gabriel. I never asked for anything. I earned it!" I turn to look at my father. "If you think me marrying into the Alvarez family will help our family, I'll do it. I'll do anything for you, Papá."

My father reaches out and takes my hand. "Thank you." He smiles. "Once again, you've proven yourself." He releases me and sits straighter in his chair. "Gabriel, it's been decided you will marry Lucia Alvarez. You will not take my place when I step down."

"Papá?"

He holds up a hand to silence him. "Gabriel, I failed you. You will do this to appease me and as penance for fucking with your sister's business. And you will *never* run our people over the border again."

Gabriel slumps in his seat. "You did this," he whispers.

I open my mouth to respond, but my father pins me with a look, silencing me. "No, son, *you* did this." He claps his hands loudly. "Now, you will smile when we tell your mother the good news, and you will appear happy."

"And if I don't?"

"I will cut you from this family. There will be no wedding and you will have nothing."

Gabriel snaps his head up and stares at our father. "You wouldn't."

"I've never lied to you before. I'm not about to start now."

My father and I stand, towering over Gabriel. Tears well in his eyes, and I look away with disgust.

Such weakness.

He was handed the brass ring without having to work for it and now … now he'll get nothing. Passed over for a woman. No one will respect him.

Instead of me being the brood mare, we have our stud. This is so fitting for Gabriel. All show and little promise.

Chapter 18

CREED

My chapter of the Royal Bastards has a diverse business portfolio. We own several strip joints, but our most profitable club is Heelz. We pay certain members of law enforcement to overlook some of our endeavors. They get paid well, but now I'm being fucked over by someone we pay *very* well. Schultz has become greedy, and the doors to Heelz are closed as he tries to renegotiate his deal. I'm sitting in the empty club waiting for him to arrive.

Heelz has been in operation for six months. We have only the best girls working this place—high-class strippers—and, for a price, you get to play with them. Prostitution is an ugly world. No one is doing anything they don't want to do. Hell, our best act doesn't even have sex with the customers. Kandy works the pole better than any I've seen, and the place is packed every night she performs.

Schultz wants a better cut. I don't like police who betray their badge. Sure, it's a necessity for someone like me, but none of my men would betray me for a dollar. Schultz and others like him are bottom feeders.

Winchester is in the wings of the stage, keeping out of sight. If shit hits the fan, he'll do whatever he needs to do to protect me. The only lights on are the ones highlighting the booze and a few around the stage. It gives the club an intimate feeling, and I wonder if Devil has ever stepped into a place like this.

I can't imagine a woman from a small country town would even know where a strip club is located. Once again, she invades my thoughts.

Stretching out my legs, I cross them at the ankles, pick up my drink, and swirl the whiskey around in the glass. The inside of the club is painted dark red. The bar is black, as are the seats and tables in the room. Each table has a small lamp in the center to offer ambient light when the girls are on stage. The poles around the room are brass, and the waitresses wear gold bikini tops and shorts when they're working the floor. The outfits leave nothing to the imagination.

"He's late," Winchester announces, his voice even louder than normal in the empty building.

"Yeah. He's a dick."

Winchester chuckles. "Wait. I'm looking at the security cams and a car has pulled into the lot."

"Is it him?"

"Not a cop car. Door's opening. Yeah, it's him."

"Be ready."

A tall man enters the club. He looks around the room, and when his eyes land on me, he walks toward my table.

"You're late," I say loudly.

"Crime never sleeps. I was on a call." He sits opposite me.

"Schultz, yeah?"

"Yes, and you must be Creed."

Grinning, I throw my arms wide. "The one and only."

"You're kind of a legend at the station."

"How so?"

"Everyone knows you killed Jimmy the Knife."

"If that were true, I would have been charged and sent to prison."

Jimmy the Knife moved here from Chicago and thought he was going to take over what was mine. I put him in the ground along with a few of his men, and the mob never sent anyone else to take his place. Violence is sometimes the best answer.

Schultz laughs. "How'd you do it?"

I ignore his probing and get right to the point. "What do you think of Heelz?"

He raises his brows and looks around. "It seems

nice. Better than some of the clubs I've been to."

"So, you frequent strip clubs?"

"Yeah."

I uncross my ankles and sit straighter in my chair. "What's the one thing strip clubs have in common?"

He shrugs. "Strippers?"

"Yeah, those and ..." I pause for a long moment. "Fucking customers!" I shout.

Schultz doesn't flinch at my outburst. "Pay me what you owe me, and you'll have them."

Either he's a fool or he has balls of steel.

"We had a deal."

"I'm changing the deal."

"We don't renegotiate."

Schultz nods, and his lips turn down at the corners of his mouth as he looks around the empty club. "Well, I guess you don't reopen."

Something inside me snaps. I stand, flip over the table, grab this worthless piece of shit by his shirt, and shove him to the ground.

"We aren't paying you another penny. You've been paid. You need to fulfill your end of the agreement."

"Fuck you. Without me, you can't open."

Red clouds my vision as I draw back my arm to hit him.

Schultz's eyes widen. "I'm a policeman. You can't hit me!"

Laughter rumbles out of my chest. "You're nothing but an inconvenience. You're a parasite, one I could happily pound into the ground without a second thought. You have no honor. You're nothing."

Schultz scrambles away from me and readjusts his shirt. "Well, I'm the nothing who got you shut down. I'm the nothing who wants more money."

My top lip curls in disgust. "We're not paying you any more money."

Schultz heads for the door. "Then I guess we are done here."

"Not quite."

Winchester moves out from the shadows, blocking his path. "Hey, Schultz."

The man stops dead in his tracks. "I'm a police officer. If anything happens to me, you're fucked."

"It's not like we haven't made people disappear. You mentioned Jimmy the Knife. Seems like *he* disappeared." Pulling my gun from its holster, I let it hang at my side.

Winchester smiles at the man but it's anything but friendly. He looks like a predator ready to pounce on his prey.

Schultz looks from me to Winchester. His face pales, displaying the fear he must be feeling.

"Come on, I'm a cop."

"You've said that already." I tap the gun against my leg, and Schultz tracks my movement.

"Okay, okay, forget it. We'll call it even."

"It's gone beyond that now. You fucked with our income stream. We don't like that." I take a step back and raise my Glock.

Schultz lunges for Winchester, but my guy sidesteps him and trips him up. He hits the floor hard, the thump echoing through the empty club. He flips over, his hands raised in surrender and fear etched into his features.

"I have a family!"

I shake my head. "No, you don't. You're not married. You live on West Ashley Street in a one-bedroom apartment. No wife, no children, and even your parents are dead."

I crouch down to stare him in the eyes.

"You see, Peter Schultz, we do our research. Normally, the police we do business with have connections within the community, but you? You have nothing. There's no leverage with you. All you have is your job, and you betrayed the badge the minute you took money from us. It was a mistake to get involved with you in the first place. You're no good to us or the people who employ you."

"I'm a cop!"

"Yeah, a dead one," Winchester deadpans.

Schultz rolls under one of the tables and stands, sending it flying. Winchester is there and sends the man backward with one punch. He stumbles over the upturned table and hits his head on the leg of the table, knocking himself out.

We stand over him as a wet patch spreads over his groin.

Winchester laughs. "Fucking pussy. What do we do with him now?"

"Killing cops is messy, even dirty ones like him. They'll rain down on us for taking out one of their own."

"Yeah. I was surprised when you drew your gun."

"It was clear he wasn't going to take no for an answer." I nudge him with my boot to make sure he isn't playing possum. "The only thing he has going for him is his job. What if we get photos of him in a compromised position and use them to keep him in line?"

"Girls? Drugs? What do you have in mind?"

"All of it. You seem to know all the strippers and whores around the club who'd be willing to help us."

"For a price, Crystal would suck off anyone. She's our best bet."

"Which one's Crystal?"

"Platinum blond, big tits, works here on the pole and as a server."

I shrug. "Not ringing any bells." After a while, all the strippers start to look the same.

"She did Highway and Scout at the same time."

"Yeah, yeah, I remember her. She's cute, a little

bit older. Okay, give her a call. Let's make this happen. And Winchester, give him something extra so he stays asleep."

"Will do, Prez."

Looking down at Schultz, I tilt my head. "Guess it's better than killing him. Keep him on a short leash. Make sure he knows he's fucked if he tries to get one over on us."

Winchester goes behind the bar and comes back with a little black pouch. He unzips it and pulls out a needle which is already primed.

"You keep shit behind the bar?"

"Homemade Rohypnol. Works great for customers who cause problems. One shot in their glass of booze and they are out within fifteen minutes or easy to maneuver, and they often don't remember what happened." He grins and kneels next to Schultz. "It makes my job easy."

Taking the man's arm, he pulls up his sleeve and injects the drug into his vein.

"How long will it last?"

"This dose should incapacitate him for twelve hours."

Raising my eyebrows, I gesture toward the drug. "Who makes this shit for you?"

Winchester smirks. "I do. Simple chemistry."

"We should have called you Chemist instead of Winchester."

"Nah, I'm a better shot than a chemist."

"You good here?"

Winchester puts his hands on his hips. "Help me get him to one of the VIP rooms?"

Bending at the waist, I grab Schultz under one arm and Winchester gets the other. We drag him through the club and into a VIP room where we drop his body on the floor. There's no need to be gentle with him. The man is scum.

My phone rings. I pull it out of my pocket and see Camilla's number on the screen. I think about not answering it, but she'll probably just keep calling. I answer and walk back out to the chair I was in when Schultz first entered.

"Yeah?"

"Hello, Creed. I need you to come out to the warehouse." She's all business. I guess Hector ratted me out.

"When?"

"Tomorrow night."

Before I can answer, she ends the call.

Fucking bitch.

Winchester moves closer to me. "You okay, Creed?"

"I'm so sick of being a fucking lap dog to the Diablo Cartel."

"You've been summoned?"

"Yeah."

"Problem?"

"Devil."

Winchester rubs his chin and sits opposite me. "What are you going to do?"

"Hector said she's safe as long as she's in the compound with us. I'm guessing he's told Camilla she's still alive." I suck in a deep breath. "I can't put her down."

"I could do it."

Pinning him with a scowl, I shake my head. "No. I don't want her dead. If the cartel will keep to their word, she'll be safe."

"And how are you going to keep her here forever? Isn't she here on vacation? Do you really think she'll want to stay?"

The truth is, I have no idea, but the thought of her in a shallow grave turns my stomach. There's something about her that calms my soul. Devil has her hooks in me so deep, I can't imagine letting her go. If I do, those hooks might just kill me.

I give the table a few solid taps and stand. "See you back at the compound."

"Creed, Devil might not feel the same way. Have you thought about that?"

I blatantly ignore his question. "See you later."

"Later."

Winchester might be right. Maybe I'm just a fling to Devil, but with the way I'm thinking, I don't believe that's the case. I meant it when I said she feels like home. It's been a long time since any woman has had this kind of impact on me. The last time this happened, I was nineteen, and she worked me over good. She betrayed me so badly, I've never let anyone else in, yet here I am, falling for a stranger. Worse than that, a stranger who has no idea about club life.

***

Devil is fast asleep when I climb into bed beside her. She has her long blond hair in a braid and is wearing one of my t-shirts even though she has clothes of her own now. Lying on my back, I stare at the ceiling, listening to her breathe. Devil rolls closer and puts her head on my chest and one leg over mine, as if she's done this her whole life. The scent of apples fills my nostrils, and a sense of calm envelopes me. For as long as I can remember, I've been looking for this, but if I'm forced to choose between her and the club, the club has to come first.

My chest aches at the thought, and I send up a prayer to whatever god is listening.

Do gods listen to the untamed?

Do they care?

With these thoughts in my head, I drift off to sleep.

Chapter 19

CREED

When I open my eyes, the sun is up, and my cock is in the middle of a wet dream.

Wait, this feels way too real. What the fuck is going on?

With a groan, I blow my load. Looking down, my eyes settle on Devil with my cock in her mouth. Definitely not a wet dream.

She wipes her mouth on the sheets and giggles. "Good morning."

Chuckling, I pull her up my body. "You can wake me up like that any time you like. Damn, woman, you should have woken me."

"I'm pretty sure I did." Devil kisses my chest. "I missed you last night."

"Sorry, it was late when I finally got in. Did you call your mom?"

"Yeah, she wasn't even worried about me." Devil smiles. "She told me to have a good time and not worry about anything. My mum is a bit of a wild spirit. She doesn't dwell in the past, she's always moving forward."

"You don't talk about your dad."

Devil repositions herself on the bed. "He died a long time ago. Mum and dad were already separated. He wasn't a nice man. He died alone and was buried a pauper. Dad's life wasn't a happy one, but he brought most of it on himself. It's a shame, really. He had people who were willing to love him, but he never let them." Sadness mars her beautiful features. "I don't think he ever loved anyone."

Wanting to make her feel better, I take her hand in mine. "Do you want to do your bike tour today?"

"Yes! Where are you going to get the push-bikes?"

Laughing at the ridiculous term, I crush her to me. "I don't do bicycles, but I *will* do bikes."

Devil frowns. "That makes no sense."

"It does to me. Go get dressed. Wear jeans."

"It's hot!"

"Woman, don't argue with me. Jeans."

Devil climbs out of bed and pads into the bathroom. Before she closes the door, she pokes her tongue out at me. I laugh and throw a pillow in her direction, but it bounces off the closed door.

Laughing to myself, I throw my feet over the side

of the bed and stand and stretch. I grab my phone from the bedside table and check my messages. There's nothing there, which is a rarity. Searching through my drawers, I pull out a black tee and look for underwear.

Devil walks out of the bathroom naked and holding a towel to her wet hair. I'm admiring her body when the meeting with Camilla tonight rears its ugly head in my thoughts.

"Do you like it here?"

She pulls on a black, lacy g-string and matching bra. "Sure. Everyone has been great."

"Do you miss home?"

Devil tilts her head to the side, and her eyes go to the ceiling as she thinks. "I miss certain things. Like some of the food. My mum."

"What about friends, your home, a job?"

"Creed, I'm on holiday, and I haven't been away long enough to miss anything."

"If I asked, would you stay longer?"

Her eyebrows shoot up. "You want me to stay longer?"

"Maybe."

"How about we see how the six weeks go? You might get sick of me."

I walk across the room to press a soft kiss to her lips, then pull away. "I'm going to shower. But just so I know ... Do you like it here?"

Raising up on her tiptoes, Devil kisses me back.

"So far, apart from our first encounter, it's been good."

In my heart, I wish we'd met under better circumstances, but she would never have drifted into my circle. If it hadn't been for Camilla or her mule, we never would have met. Fate can be a fickle bitch.

Turning, I head for the bathroom. Devil has a clean towel waiting for me. It's nice to have someone look after me for a change. It's been a long time since anyone has done anything for me.

Smiling, I turn on the water, lather up, and do what I need to do. I'm in and out of the bathroom in under ten minutes. When I walk out, Devil is dressed and holding a framed photograph of my mother.

"Where did you find that?" My words come out far harsher than I intend.

Devil jumps and clutches it to her chest. "I was hanging my clothes and found it the other day. And just now, when I pulled out my shirt, it slipped onto the floor."

Taking it away from her, I stare down at my mom's face. It must be at least three years since I've looked at it.

"It was in a box." I look at her sharply. "Were you snooping? If there's something you want to know, Devil, all you have to do is ask."

Her mouth gapes open, and she waves her hands

at me, flapping them in the air. "I'm sorry. I found it the first night I was here. I–"

"So you *were* snooping?"

"Creed, that's not fair." Devil runs her hands through her wet hair. "I was scared. I was looking for a gun or something I could use as a weapon."

Clamping my mouth shut, I search her face. She's telling the truth, and, in all honesty, I don't mind that she went looking. Seeing my mother's face has turned my mood sour.

Trying to not be a dick and ruin what started out as a good day, I take a breath and exhale slowly as I peer down at the woman who was my nightmare.

"It's my mother."

"She's beautiful."

Frowning, I shake my head. "On the outside, but inside, her soul was black." I let out a self-depreciating laugh. "Far blacker than mine, and that's saying something."

Devil touches my arm. "Your soul isn't black."

If she only knew the decision I had to make. Kill her to keep Camilla and the Diablo Cartel happy, or keep her here to make me happy and maybe save a tiny piece of my black soul.

"Creed?"

My eyes meet hers. "You don't belong in my world," I whisper.

Devil takes the photograph from me and puts it back inside the box before shutting the door.

Taking me by surprise, she wraps her arms around me and holds on tightly.

"That's the beauty of our arrangement. I'm not in your world, I'm only visiting."

Her words make my heart ache. I want to tell her the truth, but how do I tell an angel she's bound for hell?

Devil pulls back from me. "You promised me a tour."

Smiling, I nod. "Yeah."

Her brow furrows, but she doesn't say anything. Instead, she pulls a comb through her hair.

I get dressed. When I'm finished, I watch her braid her blond hair. With deft fingers, she has it done quickly and neatly.

"How does it look?" She turns around so I can inspect the back of her head.

"Great."

"No lumps or bumps?"

"Woman, I said it looks great."

"Yes, but men say stuff like that all the time without actually looking."

"I'm not most men. If it looked horrible, I'd say something."

She smiles. "You don't lie?"

"Not about hair."

She laughs, and the sound warms me.

"Come on, Devil, let's get going. I'm taking you out to breakfast and then we're going on your bike tour."

She moves to leave the room, but I grab her hand. She turns to face me with confusion in her eyes. "What?"

"Do you have a jacket?"

"Creed, it's hot. I'm not wearing a jacket."

"Yes, you are." I find an old denim jacket in the back of my closet. "Here."

"Really?"

I raise an eyebrow at her, and she huffs and takes it from me, reluctantly putting it on. Chuckling, I take her hand and lead her downstairs.

Reaper is sitting at one of the tables. Our eyes meet, and he dips his head to greet me. He looks tired, but I don't have time for his demons today.

As we pass him, I say, "I need you tonight. We have a meeting at six. Ask Scout to come as well."

"Diablo?"

"Yeah."

The heat of the Florida summer hits us as we walk outside and to my Harley. I've had this bike for five years. It's black and chrome and has the club logo etched on the sides of the tank. The bike looks brand new. I keep her looking pristine.

Climbing on, I hold out a hand to Devil.

She looks a little nervous as she runs her hands down her jean-clad legs. "I've never been on the back of a bike before."

"I was practically born on one. You're in safe hands."

Tentatively, she puts her hand in mine and gets on. She immediately wraps her arms around me and squeezes me tightly.

Tilting my head so I can see her, I say, "Relax. It's been a long time since I've dropped a bike, and I've never dropped this one."

"Dropped?"

"As in, had an accident. It's also why you're wearing a jacket and jeans. If we have an accident, it'll protect you. Road rash isn't fun."

"You are not making me less nervous."

Laughing, I start the Harley. Devil jumps, and I pat her hands. "You're going to love it."

"We will see," she replies with tension in her voice.

When I pull away, Devil plasters herself against my back. It takes about five minutes for her to relax. Finally, she leans back and slowly releases her death grip. She rests her hands on my waist, and as we make our way to my favorite diner, I can't help but think how right it feels to have her on the back of my bike.

She's a natural.

Devil moves with the bike like she's done this her whole life.

When we finally stop and I turn off the Harley, Devil hugs me from behind.

"That was awesome!"

Chuckling, I twist in my seat. "Not so bad?"

Her face turns a lovely shade of pink. "Not at all. It was fun."

Winking at her, I bob my head to signal she can climb off.

Embarrassment crosses her features as she begins to awkwardly dismount. "Oh, right."

"I'm glad you liked it."

"Do you think we could have sex on it?"

Her question takes me by surprise, and I stumble as I lift my leg over the bike. "We could try."

Devil's shade of pink turns red. "I thought you'd already tried it by now."

"Uh, no. But for you, I'm willing to give it a go."

"So ..." She looks around as if she doesn't know what to say. "Do you know anyone here?"

Looking over the bikes parked out front, I recognize Highway's old black Harley, Shovelhead. He's repaired it many times, but she still leaks oil way too frequently.

"Yeah, this is a hangout for us."

Slinging my arm over her shoulders, I guide us inside. About a dozen or so of the MC members are in here, and some of them have their ol' ladies with them. Sitting in a booth at the far end of the diner is Fingers, the club's computer hacker, and Nerd, his woman. Both of them have skills on a computer I can't even begin to comprehend. Fingers supplies us with IDs, hacks any system, and has a back door into the local police department's computer network. He always knows when we're going to be raided, and we're never unprepared.

A few of the boys say hello, and some of them seem surprised I'm with a woman. I keep us moving until we come to Fingers and Nerd.

"Mind if we join you?"

Fingers nearly chokes on his coffee, but Nerd smiles and answers, "Sure, Prez. Pull up a seat."

Even if I have someone with me, I normally sit at the counter. It's unusual for me to sit in a booth.

"Fingers, Nerd, this is Devil."

Nerd smiles broadly. "Hey, Devil."

Devil slides into the booth, and I join her.

"G'day. I'm assuming your real name isn't Nerd, like mine isn't Devil?"

"An Aussie. And no, but it's what everyone calls me. My ol' man and I are wicked good with computers."

"Okay, that makes sense."

"How'd you get Devil?"

"I hit Reaper over the head with a lamp, so he christened me a Tasmanian Devil, but I've never been to Tassie. And I'm no devil."

Nerd laughs, but Fingers looks at Devil with an open mouth.

"You hit Reaper over the head and made it out alive?" Fingers' eyes bulge as he leans forward.

Reaper and Fingers are on opposite ends of the spectrum. They don't mingle, but they respect each other. Reaper is a killing machine while Fingers is on another playing field altogether. At least Nerd can hold a conversation. Fingers can, if he's talking computer-speak.

Devil nods. "I know, right? The guy is scary. He laughed."

"He laughed?" Fingers' eyes come to me.

"They made up. Reaper is cool with her." I snag a menu and hand it to Devil.

Hitting a patched-in member on home turf isn't something anyone can expect to get away with, but I don't want Fingers making a big deal out of it and scaring Devil.

"What's good?" Devil picks up a menu.

I put my arm around her shoulders. "Everything."

"Biscuits and gravy?" Devil's mouth turns up on one side.

"My favorite," Nerd replies.

"Wait, you eat biscuits *with* gravy?"

All three of us ogle her like she's grown a second head.

"Yes?" Nerd looks between us. "Mine should be here soon."

Devil scrunches up her nose. "I might wait to see what that looks like." She gives me all of her attention. "What are you having?"

"Biscuits, gravy, sausages, and eggs over medium."

Fingers' and Nerd's meals arrive, and the server turns to us.

"Hey, Creed. The usual?"

"Can you give us a minute?"

"Sure. You want coffee while you wait?"

"Yeah."

"How about you, honey? Do you want coffee?"

Devil beams up at her. "Yes, please, black."

The server stares down at me. "A girl after your own heart, hey? I'll be back."

Devil leans over and inspects Nerd's plate. "They're not biscuits, they're scones." She shifts her gaze to me. "What's the white stuff?"

Chuckling, I take her hand in mine. "They're biscuits, not scones, and it's breakfast gravy."

"It's white."

"It's supposed to be."

Devil looks back at Nerd's plate.

"Did you want to try it?" Nerd pushes her plate closer to her.

"No... I ... Do you guys have pancakes? Like, normal-looking pancakes?"

Our server returns to the table. "We sure do, honey. Do you want maple syrup and a side of bacon?" She puts a cup in front of each of us and pours the coffee before topping of our tablemates' cups.

"Bacon and pancakes?"

"Uh-huh," our server replies as she holds pen to paper.

"No, just the pancakes and syrup."

"Okay. Creed?"

"Just my usual."

She writes mine down and walks away. Devil is staring at the food on the table.

"What's wrong?" I run my thumb over her knuckles.

"Biscuits in Australia are sweet, and we have them with coffee or tea."

"Ahh, cookies."

"Yeah, we call them that too. And gravy is brown. We don't do white gravy. And we don't do pancakes with maple syrup and bacon."

Fingers snickers. "Aussies are weird."

"No, no, no. It's not us, mate. It's you."

Nerd barks out a laugh. "I'm afraid you're out numbered, Devil."

A hand lands on my shoulder, and I lean my head back to find Winchester behind me.

"You got a minute, Prez?"

Sliding out of the booth, I look down at Devil. "You okay here?"

"Yes."

"I won't be long. Don't eat my breakfast."

"You have nothing to worry about."

Laughing, I follow Winchester outside. When he

turns around, the laughter dies on my lips.

"Problem?"

"Schultz."

"What is it now?"

Winchester shuffles from side to side. "He's dead."

Looking up at the sky, I put my hands on my hips. "How?"

"I think the head injury was worse than we thought, or maybe he had a reaction to the drug."

"Fuck," I say through gritted teeth.

"What do you want to do?"

"Make him disappear." I fix my gaze on him. "This can't blow back on us."

"I know."

"Yeah, well, make sure it doesn't."

Winchester makes no move to leave and dips his chin toward Devil in the diner. "What are you going to do about her?"

"And this is your business because?"

"I'm not questioning you, Creed. I know you. You're a tough bastard who doesn't need anyone. But I see the way you are with her. You're different."

"I'm waiting for you to get to the point," I reply angrily.

"Maybe a dead cop in Diablo territory could work in our favor?"

My anger dissipates and is replaced with

curiosity. "How?"

"Do you think you could get some DNA from Camilla?"

Deep in thought, I fix my eyes on Devil. It'd be easy to fuck Camilla again and take her underwear as a trophy, but the thought makes my blood run cold.

I scrub a hand over my face and sigh. "What's your plan?"

"We could implicate her in his death, and she'd have to leave. Rumor has it she's next in line for the crown."

"Nah, it'll go to Gabriel."

Winchester laughs. "Not likely. Word on the street is he's being used as a gift to the Alvarez family. They'd want to keep her safe, so she'd get called home."

"What kind of gift?"

"They're marrying him off."

"No fucking way."

Winchester nods. "Yep. So … can you do it?"

"Even if I *could* do this, Hector would probably take over. He's just as bad as Camilla. I don't see how this helps us."

He puts his hands in his pockets. "Hector can be reasoned with, but Camilla wants you for herself. If she finds out Devil is alive and living with you, she'll rain hell down on us."

"But if Camilla's not here, she'll have no idea and

Hector might reconsider?"

"Maybe."

"Except I've been summoned, so she might already know."

"Which means your woman is as good as dead."

"Yeah."

"I'll put the cop on ice. Let's see how tonight pans out."

It's a crazy idea, but if I could let Devil have a normal life back in Australia instead of being stuck here with me, it's worth considering.

"Make sure the cop isn't tied to us."

"Already working on it. Catch you later."

Trying to hide my unease, I walk back into the diner and slide in beside Devil.

She places a hand on my knee. "Everything okay?"

"Yeah."

Devil tilts her head and quirks a brow in my direction. "I stole one of your sausages."

With a smirk, I say, "You'll pay for that later."

Chapter 20

CREED

Today was the most fun I've had since taking over as president of the Royal Bastards. Devil and I explored parts of Jacksonville I didn't know existed. She's fun to be around, easy to talk to, and makes me happy. The thought makes me frown as we pull into Camilla's parking lot. There are five cars here, which makes me glad I had the forethought to bring Scout and Reaper with me.

"Stay frosty, yeah?" I say as I dismount.

"Always," Scout replies.

Reaper merely dips his chin.

When we enter the warehouse, Hector is just inside the door, waiting for us.

"Creed." He nods in greeting and looks at my men behind me. "Could I have a minute, alone?"

I gesture to Reaper with a flick of my head, and

they proceed ahead of me.

I wait to speak until they are out of earshot. "Is there a problem?"

Hector lowers his voice. "Did you get rid of our problem?"

"No, the problem is still at our clubhouse."

Hector smiles, but it doesn't reach his eyes. "If she finds out …"

"You didn't tell her?"

Hector rolls his eyes. "I see no reason to tell her. You've never let us down before."

His comment surprises me. We've had two shipments of heroin come up short. This would definitely mean I've let them down.

"What do you want, Hector?"

"Simple. You do what I want, when I want, and your pet stays safe."

My lip curls up in a sneer. "And if I don't?"

"Well, let's just say the Diablo Cartel won't be pleased with you."

Realization hits me like a freight train. I lean toward him, invading his personal space, but Hector doesn't move. "*You're* the reason the shipments are short."

Hector smiles. "Not so dumb after all."

"Why would you risk yourself and your position for a few bricks?"

The smile dies on his lips. "It wasn't me, but it's someone close to me."

"It will look bad for you if Camilla finds out."

Hector locks eyes with me. "Worse for you if she finds out about your pet."

"Seems we're at an impasse."

"It won't happen again. The issue has been resolved."

"And my pet isn't an issue either."

Hector holds out his hand. "May Camilla never find out about either of us."

We grip hands firmly and shake on it before making our way inside. I follow Hector upstairs to go to Camilla's office, but Reaper meets me at the landing and leans in close to my ear.

"Did he tell you who's here?"

Casting a glance at Hector, I shake my head. "No."

"Mateo Sanchez."

Great. Didn't see this coming.

I sigh. "Where's Scout?"

Reaper points over his shoulder with his thumb at the closed door of Camilla's office. Hector knocks twice and opens the door.

Inside, we find Mateo sitting behind Camilla's desk. "Ahh, Creed! So good to see you." Mateo stands and embraces me in a hug.

This feels strange. Mateo and I have always had a good working relationship, but we have never been close.

"Mateo."

He holds me at arm's length. "You look good.

Whoever she is, keep her."

Hector barks out a laugh, and I pin him with a scathing look. Scout moves to stand next to Hector and smirks at me.

"Ahh, so there *is* someone?"

Not daring to look at Camilla, I reply, "Something like that."

Mateo releases me and wags a finger in my face. "A good woman is like a fine wine, they get better with age. If she complements you, don't let her get away."

Camilla glares at me with barely controlled rage, but when her father turns around, she smiles widely and nods. If nothing else, Camilla is a great actress.

"Come, Creed. Sit. Let us talk."

Mateo returns to his place behind the desk, and I sit on one of the armchairs in front of it. He's dressed in a black suit with a cream silk shirt, looking every bit the drug dealer. Mateo wears many gold rings, and his hair is slicked back. For an older man, he's fit, tanned, and reminds me of a snake, always ready to strike.

Camilla sits on a chair beside her father. Tonight, she has on a black pantsuit and a blouse buttoned up to her neck. She's showing no skin, no cleavage—nothing to embarrass her father. Her ruby-red lips and nails are the only signs of femininity.

"Rumor has it congratulations are in order."

Mateo looks puzzled as his brows crease. "I'm sorry?"

"Gabriel is getting married?"

Mateo's lips turn down for an instant. "Yes. My son is getting married." He looks at Camilla. "If only my daughter was as lucky in love."

"Indeed," I reply.

"Hector, we need drinks for our friends," Mateo announces jovially.

Hector moves to a cabinet and holds up a bottle of tequila. "Or would you prefer whiskey?"

"Pfft! Real men drink tequila. One for all of us," Mateo orders.

"Not for my men."

Camilla smiles. "Still don't trust us, Creed?"

"It's not about trust. They have work to do later. I need them to be sharp."

Mateo points at me. "This is what I like about you. Always thinking ahead."

Hector places glasses of tequila in front of Mateo, Camilla, and me.

I raise my glass to the others. "To all our good fortunes."

"To working together for a long time." Mateo holds up his glass. "Salud!"

I throw back the drink and slam the glass on the desktop, shattering it into a thousand pieces.

Mateo laughs loudly. "Hector! Get him another."

With a tight smile, Hector grabs another glass for me and refills the other two. Without being told, Hector scoops up the broken shards into his hand.

"Maldicón!" Hector hisses as crimson runs through his fingers.

Mateo hands him a handkerchief. "Go clean yourself up."

He quickly leaves the room, and Scout follows closely behind him.

"Can we talk freely?" Mateo fixes Reaper with a probing gaze.

I clear my throat. "Mateo, this is Reaper. He's my second in charge. You can say whatever you wish."

He stares at Reaper for a moment, then directs his gaze to me. "Thank you for your help with the … shipment you encountered recently."

"All part of the service."

"It is not part of our business. It will never happen again."

"Do you know what happened to the survivors?"

Mateo takes a sip of his drink. "No." He shakes his head and looks at the desktop, seemingly absorbed in his thoughts.

Camilla places a hand on her father's arm. "My father and I are on the same page. We'd like to expand our business, and we'd like you to connect us with other chapters within your organization. For a fee, of course."

"Of course."

"Camilla will fill you in on all the details. For now, I'd just like to reinforce our business agreement and tell you we appreciate your calm under what, I am sure, were extreme circumstances."

"Mateo, we've known each other long time. As always, the Royal Bastards are happy to be in business with the Diablo Cartel."

Mateo smirks. "But?"

"We don't answer to you. It's a business agreement, and I don't like being told what to do." Camilla squirms under my gaze, and I'm sure she's worried I'll say something to put her in a bad light with her father.

Mateo frowns. "If Camilla has overstepped, I apologize. It won't happen again."

Standing, I hold out my hand to Mateo, and he rises from his chair.

"Good seeing you, Mateo."

"You too, Creed."

I dip my head to him and then Camilla. Turning on my heel, I leave the room with Reaper at my side. We keep going until we hit the parking lot.

"Where the hell is Scout?"

Reaper shrugs. "He trailed after Hector like a puppy chasing a bone."

Scout jogs out of the warehouse with a shit-eating grin on his face.

"What's got you looking so happy?" Reaper rubs the back of his neck.

Scout shakes his head. "Later."

***

The three of us pull into the compound and park near the fire pit. Reaper dismounts first, and his eyes are glued to something I can't yet see. Moving to stand next to him, I follow his gaze. Lucy's sitting on Highway's knee, her head thrown back in laughter. Reaper's lip twitches, and his hand forms a fist.

"You've got it bad, don't you?"

Without looking at me, he says, "She makes life easier." His nostrils flare. "She makes me better."

"Then why are you standing here with us?" Scout asks.

Reaper looks at me.

A growl rumbles deep in my chest. "If you hurt her, I will put–"

"I won't. And if I do, I'll take myself out."

"Jesus, this conversation took a dark turn," Scout mutters.

Reaper raises a brow at me as if asking for permission, and I nod. He stalks toward Lucy, and she hastily stands. He says nothing, bends and puts her over his shoulder, and carries her into the clubhouse.

"Reaper!" Highway shouts, but he makes no move to chase after them.

Scout turns to me with a wide grin on his face. "So … are you going to ask me what I was doing at the warehouse?"

"Scout, just tell me."

He reaches into his pocket and pulls out a bloody handkerchief. "I got Hector's blood and some glass."

"Why the fuck would we want that?"

"Well, I was talking to Win, and he suggested if you couldn't seal the deal with Camilla, I should try. But seeing as her dad was there, I couldn't see that happening, so I got Hector's."

He's clearly pleased with himself, but right now, I can't see how this will help us.

I sigh and pinch the bridge of my nose. "What are you going to do with it?"

"I'm going to give it to Win."

"You do that." Slapping him on the arm, I turn to walk into the clubhouse, but a flash of blond hair near Highway catches my eye and stops me in my tracks.

Devil is talking to Justice, but he's standing a little too close. He hands her a bottle, and she takes a sip before handing it back to him. Justice smiles at her and drinks from it as well. He's been a good soldier, always able to sense danger before things turn to shit. He laughs at something she says, but then he sees me striding toward them and he takes a few steps back from her. Justice nods in my direction, and Devil turns around. Her whole face lights up into a smile as she jogs toward me and throws her arms around me.

"You're home!"

Devil kisses me as wolf whistles pierce the air. Our tongues duel for a moment, and the taste of Fireball hits me.

"You're drunk."

"I'm tipsy, not drunk."

My gaze lands on Justice. "You were flirting."

Devil frowns. "Was not."

"I saw you."

"I've been waiting for you."

"And what were you waiting for?"

Devil entwines her fingers with mine and tugs me toward the clubhouse. "Let me show you."

With the promise of once again getting between her thighs, I let Devil pull me through the clubhouse and up to my room.

Once we make it over the threshold, she walks backward as she peels off her clothes. It's sexy as hell. Shutting the door, I lock it and kick off my boots. Devil shimmies out of her jeans and then trips, landing flat on her ass.

"Are you okay?" Holding out a hand to her, I laugh.

Devil squints at me. "Not funny."

"It's kind of funny." My hand drops to my side.

Her lips turn down as she pouts. "I'm trying to be sexy."

Kneeling beside her, I cup her face. "You *are* sexy. No need to try."

Devil leans in and sucks my bottom lip between her teeth.

"You *make* me sexy."

Chuckling, I help her stand and step out of the jeans tangled around her feet. With one arm around her waist and the other holding onto her neck, I kiss her. Devil's body responds and arches into me.

"Need more," she moans.

"What do you need?"

Her face flushes red. "I need you."

I'm the president of an MC. I'm not nice. I'm not sweet. I am good at what I do, and even though she's uncomfortable saying the words, it's important to me that she submits and tells me what she wants. Instructing her to keep her eyes on me is another way I need for her to let me dominate her.

Stepping back, Devil bites her lip as confusion crosses her face.

"What do you want?" I place my hand under her chin and run my thumb over her lips.

"You."

"If you want me to make you feel good, you're going to have to spell it out."

In one fluid movement, she removes her bra and panties. "Do you want me?"

"Yes."

Undoing my belt, I let my jeans fall to the ground. My cock is hard and stands at attention. Devil places her hand around my shaft. I hiss at her touch, but this isn't about me.

Gripping her arm, I force her movements to stop. "Tell me."

"I want you."

"I know that. How?"

Realization spreads across her face, and I can almost read her mind as she finally figures out what I mean.

Devil sits on the bed and spreads her legs. She cups a breast with one hand and tangles the other in her hair.

"Creed, I want your face between my legs, and I want you to eat m-me." She stammers on the last word as uncertainty crosses her pretty features.

Dropping to my knees, I crawl toward her. I trace my hands up her legs and spread them wider. Starting at her knee, I pepper kisses up to her thigh.

"Like this?"

"Almost," she whispers.

As I move to the other leg, I blow on her pussy. She gasps, and I kiss from her knee to her pussy, settling on the sensitive bundle of nerves above her entrance.

"Like this?"

"Yes."

"Eyes on me, Devil."

"Always."

As a reward, I bury my face in her slick folds, sucking and teasing the very depths of her. Devil clutches me to her, riding my face, her moans growing louder until she screams my name. Devil falls backward on the bed, and I kiss my way up her body. She wraps a leg around me, and I position myself to enter her tight heat.

Slowly, I push inside her, and she shudders at the new invasion. I pull out and do it again, and Devil rocks her hips in sync with my movement.

"Faster, Creed."

Pounding into her, I take my pleasure from her. Devil's eyes are glazed with lust as she watches me move in and out of her. Sparks of electricity shoot through my limbs as I try to make this last longer.

"Let go," she whispers, as though she can read my mind.

Hearing those words tips me over the edge. As I seat myself inside her as far as I can go, my orgasm washes through me. Never before has a woman made me come so hard for so long. With a growl against her neck, I realize I'm never letting Vivian Lewis, my Devil, go home.

Chapter 21

DEVIL

Rolling over, I reach out only to find our bed is empty. Cracking an eyelid, I look around the room. Creed isn't here. There's a note on the bedside table with a bottle of water and some Advil. It's much like the first day I found myself here, but I'm not scared this time. I'm happy.

> *Devil,*
> *I'm downstairs. Come down when you're ready and I'll cook you breakfast or lunch, depending on the time.*
> *Creed*

Turning onto my back, I smile up at the ceiling. This holiday is nothing like I'd imagined. Never in a million years did I think I'd meet a man like him.

He's a beast.

My beast.

A man who can't seem to get enough of me.

I'm sure he has no idea what I'm saying half the time, but he never makes me feel less than or stupid. Picking up my phone, I send my mum a hello with a bunch of kissy face emojis and get out of bed to head for the shower.

Tipsy sex is messy sex, but I swear he made me melt. He always makes sure I'm taken care of, and not just in the bedroom.

In the bathroom, I shower, dry myself off quickly, and dress in shorts and a tank top. It all takes less than ten minutes, then I hurry downstairs. My flip-flops make thwacking sounds as I make my way to the bottom. Rounding the corner, I see Creed and make a beeline for him.

But there's something in his stance. Tension. It's not until I'm nearly upon him that I see a woman with long, thick, dark hair.

She's beautiful.

Her dress hugs her curves, accentuating them. Her lips are full and painted red. This woman looks like something out of a fantasy, and she's staring at Creed with a look that's less than polite. She appears almost hungry.

Reaper sees me coming and holds up a hand, but I keep going.

Creed is mine.

I don't share.

Slipping a possessive arm around his waist, I smile and hold out a hand to her.

"G'day, I'm Devil."

The woman gasps and looks from Creed to me, the crease between her brows marring her gorgeous face. She looks at my outstretched hand and then back at Creed.

"Who is this?" she hisses.

Creed wraps an arm around me. "Camilla, this is Devil."

"Hi," I say meekly, giving her a small wave since she won't shake my hand.

"What's your *real* name?" Camilla demands.

Creed tenses, and she sees it.

"Well?" her voice rises as she bores holes into me with her pretty, brown eyes.

"D-Devil."

Camilla pokes Creed in the chest. "What the fuck is this?"

He holds up a hand to her and looks at me. "Go wait in the kitchen."

"No!" Her beautiful face begins to twist into something ugly. "She's supposed to be dead."

"Diablo Cartel," I whisper.

Laughter sounding more like a cackle escapes her. "*This* is the reason you've not come to see me? *Her*?"

"Leave it alone, Camilla."

She shakes her head. "If you can't do it, I can arrange for it to be done."

"She's no threat to you."

"I'm not, I promise. Ria and I got our bags mixed up. I had no idea hers had your drugs in it."

Creed flinches at my words, and Camilla's mouth falls open.

"Did you hear what she just said to me? You had *one* job, Creed. This ... this woman is a complication you don't need."

"I'm right here." I step away from Creed and out of his embrace. "I'm going home in a few weeks. I won't tell anyone."

"No, of course you won't, because you'll be dead."

Creed steps in front of me. "We have a deal with Hector."

"Hector?" Camilla turns and looks at a man behind her. "Get. Hector. Now."

He leaves the building, and she slowly turns around with a fake, creepy smile on her lips.

"Did he tell you he fucked me?" Her words take me by surprise, and I take a step back. "From your slack-jawed expression, I think not."

"Camilla," Creed growls, "it was a one-time thing, and you know it."

Moving around Creed so I can get a better look at her, I say, "We're together now. Whatever you think you had can't have been very good if it was only one time."

Camilla's face flushes red as she opens her purse and pulls out a small gun. "What did you say to me?"

The clubhouse goes completely silent. It's as though all the noise disappeared the minute her gun appeared.

The man from the mall enters the building. His eyes immediately go to her gun, and he walks toward her.

"Did you know she was still alive? Did you?" Camilla's voice is bordering on hysteria.

"Yes, we made a deal."

She looks at him with disgust. "Who gave you that right?"

"You did when you went home to your father. You left me in charge."

Camilla's face turns to stone, and she looks at me with dead eyes. "What was the deal?"

Hector takes a deep breath. "She either stays here at the compound with Creed, or she goes in the ground."

My eyes shift to Creed, and his lips turn down at the corners. He looks at me with eyes full of worry. He doesn't dispute his claims, looks back at Camilla, and nods.

So I'm nothing more than a plaything until it's time for me to leave?

No.

He said he felt it.

The pull to him is strong. It can't be a lie. I know I mean more to him.

Camilla waves her gun at me. "What's it to be, Devil? Are you staying here indefinitely, or are we going to feed you to the gators?"

Where I thought she was beautiful, I now see she's a horrible, evil thing with pretty skin. There's not a hint of real beauty to her. She's a sculpted, well put together robot. One I assume is used to getting what she wants.

"I'm with Creed. Where he goes, I'm by his side." My words come out far stronger and with more conviction than I feel.

A smile flashes across Creed's face, but he quickly quells it.

"Not good enough," Camilla hisses as she raises her gun.

To me, it looks like a prop or something a child would play with.

"I gave them my word," Hector says quietly.

A man walks into the clubhouse and sidles up beside Creed.

"Is there a problem, Prez?"

"Camilla, you know Winchester, my Sergeant at Arms, don't you?"

She looks at him as though he's a bug. "Yes."

Winchester smirks. "Seems your man here, Hector, killed a cop. But don't worry, we cleaned it up. It'd be bad for business if they found the body."

Hector's face flushes red. "I did no such thing!"

"Killing cops is bad for business," Creed states with a grin.

"What the fuck is going on?" Camilla demands.

Creed cracks his neck from side to side. "It's simple, Camilla. A cop died, and from what we can gather, Hector, your right hand, did it."

Camilla looks at her man as he adamantly shakes his head.

"I don't believe you." Her words hang in the air.

"See, that's the thing. It doesn't matter. What *does* matter is, we have the body of a cop with Hector's blood on it." Winchester gazes at Hector with a smirk on his face.

"Why do I care?" Her gaze bounces from Winchester to Creed.

"It's simple, really. We'll honor Hector's agreement and keep Devil here, and in return, we won't tell the police where the body is. You know how cops are when you kill one of their own. They don't eat, they don't sleep. They exist to tear you down. That means no drugs, which, in turn, means no money." Creed raises his chin and straightens his shoulders.

"But I didn't kill anyone."

Creed smiles at Hector. "How's your hand feeling?"

Hector looks at his hand, then at Creed, and resignation crosses his features. "Scout.

Fucking Scout."

Creed tips his head, and his lips turn up at the corners.

But Camilla only has eyes for me. She lowers the gun and places the other hand on her hip. "Tell us, Devil, are you willing to stay here forever?"

Creed turns slightly to lock eyes with me, and when I take in the rest of the room, it feels as though everyone is holding their breath.

Am I willing to stay here forever?

Camilla tilts her head as she watches me like I'm prey. "Well?"

Closing the gap between Creed and myself, I lace my fingers with his. "We're a team." I give his hand a reassuring squeeze. "The answer is yes. I'm staying."

Camilla makes a weird gasping noise. "Oh, and how are you going to do that? Are you going to marry her?"

Creed gazes down at me. "If it comes to that, yes."

Knowing she's beaten, Camilla puts her toy gun away. Her eyes fixate on the floor. "I'll be watching."

She turns and strides out of the clubhouse. Hector dips his chin at Creed.

"Well done." Hector gives me one last look and hurries after his mistress.

Creed smiles at me, but I pull away from him. Confusion mars his features, and his eyes narrow. "Devil?"

"What if I'd said no? Would you have killed me?"

"But you didn't."

"What if I had?"

He looks around the room filled with only patched-in members and no club whores.

"I promised you when you first came here, no harm would come to you."

Straightening my shoulders, I raise my chin and look him dead in the eyes. "An easy promise to keep me placated. Did you mean what you just said?"

"No one will harm you."

"Not what I meant. How are you going to keep me here in the United States? I checked, and the longest I can stay is three months."

"If you try to leave, the Diablo Cartel will kill you."

Putting a hand on my hip, I point at him. "How?"

Winchester laughs. "Oh, I know what she wants."

Creed looks at him and shrugs.

"It's green."

Creed's eyes grow wide. "Money?"

Reaper barks out a laugh. "Not money. A green card."

Creed whirls around and looks at me sharply. "You want to get married?"

Turning my back on him, I walk toward the kitchen. "Want has nothing to do with it. It's the only way for me to keep breathing."

Pushing open the doors, I stand in the kitchen

alone, waiting for him to pursue me. Through the closed door, I hear laughter. Moving farther into the room, I stand in front of the refrigerator. The doors swing wide, and Creed strides into the room. He stalks over to me, and I instinctively move away from him, but he keeps coming until my backside slams into the kitchen bench.

He tangles his hands in my hair and kisses me. This isn't a soft, sweet kiss or even a sexy one. This kiss is different. It's possessive and soul binding.

"If I hadn't made the bargain with Hector, would you have stayed willingly?"

"What does it matter?"

"I can get you home if you want to go. But if you want to stay and belong to me ..." His eyes search mine. "I'd marry you a hundred times over."

All the air rushes from my lungs. "I love you."

Creed smiles and dips his head to kiss the corner of my mouth. "Vivian Lewis, I love you." He kisses my nose. "*And* I'm keeping you."

Reaper
The Royal Bastards MC Jacksonville FL

More books
TO CHECK OUT

The Savage Angels MC Series

Savage Stalker Book 1
Savage Fire Book 2
Savage Town Book 3
Savage Lover Book 4
Savage Sacrifice Book 5
Savage Rebel (Novella) Book 6
Savage Lies Book 7
Savage Life Book 8
Savage Christmas (Novella) Book 9
Savage Angels MC Collection Books 1 – 3
Savage Angels MC Collection Books 4 – 6
Savage Angels MC Collection Books 7 – 9
Savage Angels MC Collection Books 1 - 9

The MacKenny Brothers Series
An MC/Band of Brothers Romance

Kathleen Kelly

Spark Book 1
Spark of Vengeance Book 2
Spark of Hope Book 3
Spark of Deception Book 4
Spark of Time Book 5
Spark of Redemption Book 6
Spark: MacKenny Brothers Series Books 1 - 3

The Tackling Series
Tackling Love Book 1
Tackling Life Book 2

Connect With ME ONLINE

Check these links for more books from
Author Kathleen Kelly

READER GROUP

Want access to fun, prizes and sneak peeks?
Join my Facebook Reader Group.
https://bit.ly/32X17pv

NEWSLETTER

Want to see what's next?
Sign up for my Newsletter.
https://www.subscribepage.com/kathleenkellyauthor

BOOKBUB

Connect with me on Bookbub.
https://www.bookbub.com/authors/kathleen-kelly

About THE AUTHOR

Kathleen Kelly was born in Penrith, NSW, Australia. When she was four, her family moved to Brisbane, QLD, Australia. Although born in NSW, she considers herself a QUEENSLANDER!

She married her childhood sweetheart, and they live in Toowoomba.

Kathleen enjoys writing contemporary romance novels with a little bit of steam. She draws her inspiration from family, friends, and the people around her. She can often be found in cafés writing and observing the locals.

If you have any questions about her novels or would like to ask Kathleen a question, she can be contacted via email:
 kathleenkellyauthor@gmail.com
or she can be found on Facebook. She loves to be contacted by those that love her books.